BROKEN SHELLS

broken shells

A NOVEL BY

Deena Bouknight

Cover Photography Deena Bouknight © 2013
Cover Design & Formatting William Baker © 2013

Light Path Publishing
4903 Westfield Road
Columbia, SC 29206

DEDICATED TO:

my family, encouragers of my work – and God, who
"establishes the work of our hands for us ..."
Psalm 90

one

Miss Whitecastle hated it when Maxine showed up late on Saturdays. Her routine was disrupted and she would have to leave the tidy organization of her desk to face an out-of-order day. She rose from planning the details of her week and grabbed the "to do" list sticky note pasted on the desk's leather writing surface. She preferred Maxine to arrive by 7 a.m. That way, she would have finished penciling in her duties and obligations with a fairly new No. 2, perfectly pointed. She was retired, but you would never know it. Each line of each calendar day was usually filled. White spaces made her anxious. It was highly important that her life have purpose and activity.

She sighed when she heard Maxine's car door slam. She stuck another sticky note on Thursday (as if she wouldn't remember her stopping point). She would have to finish her weekly schedule and pay bills after she spoke to Maxine about the flower beds and cleaning inside the house.

Miss Whitecastle made her way to the door to meet the woman who had faithfully served her for years. *Has it been 34 or 36?* It was 7:45 a.m. on a spring day in 2004, and she expected that this day's interactions with her employee to be like the hundreds of others that transpired over weeks and months and years. But this would not be like other days.

"Sorry I'm a little late, ma'am," said Maxine, instantly recognizing her employer's perturbed stance: right hand on her right hip; the other holding the door open impatiently. Regardless, Maxine smiled wide.

"The Lord kept me on my knees a little longer this mornin' ma'am. I had to praise Him for my cousin comin' back safely from his duties over in Afghanistan. Had to ask Him, too, for my aunt's healin'. Sure lots to pray for. It's been one of those weeks. Know what I mean?" She was unaffected by Miss Whitecastle's nettled disposition.

"There are just several areas that need attention …" started Miss Whitecastle, only to be interrupted.

"Oh Lordy! That's right! You got that meetin' here with the old ladi… I mean elderly ladies this week. Ya'll need to spend some time groomin' the younger girls in the ways of the church. That's right. I didn't forget. Things need to be spic, and they needs to be span around here. They'll be shinin' when I'm through. Don't you worry none." Maxine said all this loud and fast.

"Yes, Maxine, that is correct," injected Miss Whitecastle before Maxine could continue. "Some of these women have never visited my home, so I would like for the furnishings to look especially nice. Please polish all the wood, clean the front door, and use the lemon cleaner for the bathrooms and the kitchen. And then just the usual vacuuming and dusting will be fine."

"I see you got some flowers," said Maxine. "I'll get to them first while it's cooler out," she decided. "Then I'll work inside during the hot."

Words of protest began to form on Miss Whitecastle's lips as Maxine set down her purse and turned to walk toward the flower beds. She did not want Maxine tracking dirt inside her home. She stopped herself and simply made it clear, "That is fine Maxine," she called out to her, "but make certain to clean up good in the mud room sink before you come in."

"Yes ma'am," said Maxine, loudly – not turning to address Miss Whitecastle. Then, under her breath, she said, "Don't I always?"

Miss Whitecastle returned to her delicately inlaid walnut and yew wood secretary and spent the next 45 minutes filling in the Thursday, Friday, and Saturday calendar squares for the upcoming week. Each day included her self-prescribed marching orders. Sunday: 9:45 Meet Myra Leigh in the entryway to confirm lunch; 12:30 Lunch with Myra Leigh; 1:30-2:30 Rest; 2:30-3:00 Choose recipes for meeting on Tuesday; 3:30 Call Elizabeth and give her menu for meeting. And so on. Each block was filled to capacity.

She paid her bills, straightened her desk, discarded used envelopes, closed the top to the secretary, turned the key, placed the key in the what-not drawer on her phone stand, and checked the clock. She typically gave Maxine an hour before she checked on her progress. The hour was almost up. She went to the kitchen and poured Maxine a glass of sweetened iced tea in a large blue disposable cup before continuing to the outdoors. She found Maxine on both knees, a partially emptied tray of flowers beside her.

"I brought you some tea, Maxine. It looks like you have almost finished with this bed."

Maxine rose from the bed, smearing the sweat that beaded on her brow and dripped onto her eyelids with the back of her wide hand. Still bent slightly forward and facing Miss Whitecastle, she slowly straightened her back. Miss Whitecastle gasped and stumbled backward. *What is that?*

Maxine did not seem to notice her employer's sudden reaction.

Miss Whitecastle looked away from Maxine, regained herself, and then turned back and handed the soot black, aging woman the wet plastic cup of tea. She quickly glanced again at her chest.

"I have one more flat of those lipstick impatiens for you to plant around the boxwoods, Maxine," Miss Whitecastle barely managed, trying not to stare. She turned away sharply and headed back toward the front door.

"Yes, ma'am," said Maxine, oblivious. "And thank you for the tea. Mighty hot today. Mighty hot. We're not gettin' much of a spring. Moved right on into the summertime this year."

Without acknowledging Maxine's comment, Miss Whitecastle opened the front door and made her way inside. She walked directly to the air conditioning vent and put her face close to the chilling vapors. *What was that?* Maxine's sweat-soaked v-necked t-shirt had revealed a reddish organism that seemed to have attached itself in her bosom.

What did I see, really? She thought it might be a handkerchief. She had seen African American women carrying handkerchiefs when they worked.

Sometimes they tied them around their heads or their necks. Perhaps Maxine had used it to mop up the perspiration on her face and then shoved it down between her breasts to free her hands. She was certainly endowed enough for the storage of such items, entertained Miss Whitecastle.

Maybe it was the heat playing tricks on me. I also haven't been to the eye doctor in quite some time.

Suddenly feeling fatigued, she poured herself some lemonade over large squares of ice and sat down in her favorite chair, a rocker she had reupholstered in a creamy rose print chintz after her mother passed. *No. I know that I saw something that is not quite right.*

Rattled, she settled herself and closed her eyes. She was 70 and slowing down. She recognized that her body needed short bouts of rest during the day. She didn't feel nearly as energetic or spontaneous as she had even the year before. Her friends in the bridge club noticed. They were always asking if she was feeling okay. But then, most were a few years younger than she. Some of the friends who convinced her to join the bridge club were acquaintances from her Charleston youth. They had married physicians and surgeons who attended the Medical University of Charleston and then taken up residency in the State's capital. All her friends, in fact, were doctors' wives. *How had that happened?* The rest of the bridge club was made up of some women she knew from her long association with the Episcopal Church. The ladies in the club felt a sort of reverence toward Miss Whitecastle. They admired her, but pitied her at the same time. Her singleness and independence made her a mystique they could not imagine in their safe, predictable lives. Though they never mentioned it when Miss Whitecastle was present, they had quietly revisited the details of her engagement so long ago to that handsome and wealthy Joseph Barrister boy. The specifics, of course, were much too noteworthy for her child-hood peers not to share them with the Columbia set. The women speculated about the harsh breakup only days before their wedding. It was a disaster for Ellen's family, the women agreed, and it surely had led to Mr. Whitecastle's stroke within the year. No wonder poor Ellen had fled to Charlotte to be with her brother for a time, and then chosen Columbia, instead of her native Charleston, in which to settle. Miss Whitecastle's early romantic misfortune and why she had not pursued other eligible suitors had been discussed so many times that it became a sort of legend in their tight circle.

"Miss Whitecastle! Miss Whitecastle!" shrilled Maxine through the screened front door, rousing her from drifting thoughts.

"The perfume is in the air, Miss Whitecastle!" she exclaimed, holding out a handful of milky white gardenia blooms in one hand and still clutching the cup of iced tea in the other. "Ain't South Carolina's air smellin' so good? These blooms are just burstin' with that sweet, sweet smell!"

Miss Whitecastle reached out to take the stemmed flowers from the woman who had faithfully cleaned her house and maintained her garden for *yes, it was 34 years*. As she did, she strained to glimpse the thing she had seen earlier. Maxine's wet shirt clung to her, divulging the shape of an object meant to stay hidden. Miss Whitecastle could just make out the lines of what resembled a misshapen plum growing between Maxine's great breasts. As her eyes widened, they met Maxine's indignant stare.

two

The morning fog was dissipating as Daniel edged the raft into the frigid water. The spring air was losing its cool edge. As the fog rose and separated, the mountains revealed themselves – looming like great beasts guarding the river.

During the early morning van ride along narrow roads that wound through remote areas of the Blue Ridge Mountains, Daniel had instructed the women and the guide-in-training, Jon, on where to sit, how to position the oars, and what to do if someone fell overboard. The four women, all acquaintances in a Charlotte writer's group, spoke excitedly amongst themselves. None of the women, including Daniel's new girlfriend Julia and her 11-year-old daughter, Rose, had ever been white water rafting.

"It's time for the ride of your lives ladies," announced Daniel, confidently, as he settled his six-foot frame into position at the bow of the 12-foot raft. Daniel was in his element. He knew the lower French Broad, and a dozen or so other rivers up and down the East Coast. He had rafted on them and kayaked. He had been the guide on hundreds of trips. He loved the way the water smelled; loved the first ripple as the oar broke the surface; loved the exhilaration and challenge of each rough spot.

Though he grew up under the steel skyscrapers and the uncontrolled growth of Charlotte, Daniel was fortunate enough to have spent summers at various camps in North Carolina's rugged Smoky Mountains. His parents thought it would be "good for him" to trade hot asphalt and noise for new friends and wide open spaces. He married himself to the river. During summers off from college and law school, rafting was his release, his fun, and his livelihood.

"This is a relatively easy route," he explained to his female passengers. "This seven-mile stretch is mostly made up of ones and twos, but toward the end we'll hit a few three's and four's."

Seizing the opportunity to show the women what he had learned, Jon – a college student at UNC-Asheville that had befriended Daniel the previous summer – chimed in and explained the classification system for rivers: "Whitewater is classified according to its difficulty and danger," said Jon, as if reading from a textbook. "Class One water is the easiest, while Class Six water is very risky. Along this river we'll experience some pourovers and pillows, and paddle through a few rock gardens." With authority he added, "I'll point out the different features of the river along the way."

Daniel glanced at Julia. She seemed perfectly at ease. *Isn't that what first attracted me?* Even amidst hundreds of fans lined up to have her sign her debut legal thriller, *Secrets Escaped*, she was cool and relaxed. There was not a hint of pressure or nervousness. He had liked that about her instantly, and he told her so when he finally got his turn to have his copy signed. Not one to read just any book, this one captivated him. When he learned the author was a fellow Charlotte native and was going to be signing books at his neighborhood Happy Bookseller, he had been too intrigued not to attend. His "in" with her were questions regarding her research. He explained that he was an attorney and complemented her for her accuracy. Then he had asked her out for coffee afterwards. She obliged, and they had been seeing each other regularly, but cautiously, for almost two months.

"I need you to back paddle Julia," yelled Daniel, playfully, interrupting what seemed to be an intense discussion with her daughter.

"Sure," she answered, smiling at him. Once the raft's stern was turned, Julia put her oar down and continued her conversation with Rose. Julia's arm was around her daughter. The bond between them was unmistakable.

Daniel guessed that the topic must be him. Julia was excited when he asked her to go rafting for the weekend, but backed off when he suggested that it just be the two of them. Rose had only met him briefly, and he gathered she did not take kindly to anyone monopolizing her mother's time. The first time Daniel was introduced to Rose, Julia almost had to force her daughter to say hello. Without a father around, Julia told him later, Rose clung to her and was suspicious of any man she became interested in. Julia apologized for her daughter's behavior. But Daniel sensed that Julia, for her part, absorbed herself in her daughter in an attempt to make up for no father figure. He felt that the two were inexplicably joined. An obstacle, but not a road block, he decided. Reluctantly, Daniel told Julia she could invite her daughter and a few friends, this time.

The mid-morning sun began to warm the bright yellow raft and its passengers. The women pulled off their windbreakers. Small gray clouds formed above the mountain peaks. "Not to worry," Daniel responded to one of the rafter's concerns about the weather. "There may be one of those quick spring-time storms, but overall the weather is supposed to be balmy and clear today."

For more than an hour the raft drifted steadily along. Now and then a few hundred yards of choppy water would send the raft bobbing up and down. Birds of all kinds skimmed the river's edge and perched in the trees.

Turkey buzzards glided just above the tree line. The wide expanse of the water and the tremendous height of the rocks along the shore generated many, "Wow! Isn't this beautiful?" comments from the passengers. In some areas of the French Broad, it seemed like the raft was in a canyon: the mountains appeared to rise directly from the river's brim.

At times the powerful stirring of the water underneath the raft slowed, and the soothing motion of calmer waters had a serene affect on the rafters. Almost in unison, passengers took deep, contemplative breaths. During one stretch of slow-moving water, Daniel stopped the raft long enough for passengers to slide in and swim. He watched as Julia seemed to lose herself for a moment in the coolness of the river. She leaned back on her lifejacket and let the warm sun penetrate her. Her long auburn hair floated above her head. Watching her, he imagined for an instant what it must be like to be baptized in such a river, with the evil blight and sinfulness of the past washed clean away.

The moment was interrupted by the river picking up speed and rippling beneath them. Julia had to swim across a steady current to catch up to the drifting raft. Daniel and Jon slowed it somewhat with their oars. After Julia ungracefully attempted to hoist her own wet body back into the raft, Daniel moved in to assist.

three

"You seen it, ain't ya?" fired Maxine. "Lordy mercy. You seen it! I knowed you did!"

"What is it Maxine?" asked Miss Whitecastle, trying to compose herself – embarrassed that Maxine caught her gaping at her black chest.

"I don't know and I don't care. I can't do nothin' about it anyways," said Maxine indignantly.

"Maxine! Don't be ridiculous! What do you mean you can't do anything about it? You should at least get it checked out by a doctor, for goodness sake!" said Miss Whitecastle. The very second she completed the sentence, it hit her. She flinched at the chastising words she had just hurled at Maxine.

Maxine remained quiet for a moment, twirling her finger around the top of the iced tea cup, the slight remains of ice cubes clinking against the sides. She looked down at her feet, and then directly at her employer.

"I ain't got no health insurance. Never have had, 'cept that time I worked for that cannin' factory out there toward the Congaree. They gave me insurance and bonuses and overtime. I thought I was ridin' high then, but you know that place closed down.

Couldn't afford to keep no insurance. Don't gets benefits when workin' for yourself."

And then, to cut the awkwardness between them, Maxine faithfully exclaimed, "The good Lord will watch out for me. He always has and He always will. I don't think He wants me gettin' in a tizzy over such a thing. I'm just waitin' for Him to make this darn thing fall off and then I'll be just fine again. Better get back to plantin'. It's goin' to be full out summertime before you know it."

And before she could give Miss Whitecastle a chance to speak again, she set her tea cup on the kitchen counter and let the screened door bang behind her.

Miss Whitecastle put her hand to her mouth. *Oh my.* She was not certain what to think or do. She knew Maxine was not well off. *But that was just the way for most black people, wasn't it?* She did not know of any of her friends' housekeepers, gardeners, or nannies who were well to do. She heard during a bridge tournament about that new black doctor to Columbia who bought over in King's Grant, and the black prosecutor who had a big home and one for his mother next door somewhere off Sumter Highway.

However, most black people, she surmised, lived out toward Congaree or on Shop Road or in one of the city's housing developments. Maxine lived off Shop Road near the Carolina Coliseum and the Fair Grounds. She knew this because Maxine would complain every time USC played a football game or the State Fair was in town.

"It's like a whole swarm a bees trying to get into their nest at one time," complained Maxine about the traffic. "I might as well just stay here and help you do something else ma'am 'cause I'm not gettin' home with all those bees buzzin' around where my home is."

Miss Whitecastle had never been to Maxine's home. *Would I have gone if she had invited me? How many times has Maxine been to my house here ... to my beach house? Hundreds?*

Maxine shared with her once that her "people" all belonged to the Congaree River area near the Congaree Swamp, an expanse of low-lying wilderness and farmland – some of which became a National Park – just 20 miles from Columbia. Maxine told her that even though her two brothers had "hightailed it out of there" as soon as they finished school to make their way up north, she made it clear that she was part of the area and it was part of her and nothing would change that fact.

Maxine recited the story of her heritage, how it had been passed down and down, until it got to her. The Congaree Indians were there first, but the smallpox wiped most of them out in 1698. She told how her great great grandmother and great great grandfather were brought to the Congaree by John Wilkes, who owned a large plantation in Virginia. He had purchased the land around the swamp from a South Carolina cousin and planned to log some of it and graze cattle on the grasses grown on the nutrient-rich soil. But first dikes had to be built to keep some of the floodwaters from the Congaree River at bay. Maxine said it was around 1848 when Wilkes carried some of his healthiest slaves, including her great great grandmother and great great grandfather, to South Carolina to do the work.

"And don't you know it was hot, hot, hot, and those mosquitoes were bitin'," expressed Maxine. "Yes ma'am. Those mosquitoes were probably feastin' on my poor great great grandmama and great great granddaddy."

She continued, "Well, after the War ended, they just didn't go back to Virginia. Wasn't nothin' there for them anyways. They were free, and that low land around the Congaree was cheap. They just worked 'til they could buy them some. So that's where they stayed, and that's where my other grandparents, my parents, and where I was born, and that's where I plan to be buried."

Maxine never tired of sharing her heritage with Miss Whitecastle. Sometimes she would talk on and on, not caring if Miss Whitecastle was even listening.

"It's the land of the giants, you know," Maxine would say. "Those loblolly pines reach so high you can't see the tops. I've never been to those big churches over there in Europe, but I think they must leave you feelin' like you do in the Congaree. Like I'm just a little person next to God's great creations. Makes you want to be quiet, just like when you're in His house.

"None of us never was quite sure about those Cyprus knees. Curious, those things are. Have you ever seen them before, Miss Whitecastle? Aren't they odd? Some think they are new trees that never went anywhere. Others say they are roots that went down toward hell, didn't like it down there, and are coming back up toward heaven. Me and Louise and Bessy, we used to sit on them and pretend they were our school stools and we was in an outdoor classroom.

"But oh Lord, that switchgain grew like crazy in that ol' swamp, and if you don't think that makes the best switches in the world! Every momma in the Congaree knows about switchgain, and that's the first thing they tell you to go for when they're lookin' to punish you on your backside. I didn't get switched too much, but my poor brothers did. That's probably why they lit out of there as soon as they could. Bad memories 'bout switchgain."

Once, when Miss Whitecastle sat engrossed in a book of Carl Sandburg's poetry she had been given by a Flat Rock acquaintance as a Christmas present, Maxine started in: "You can have your Sandburgs and your Emersons. I can tell you I grew up with the only pure poetry there is, and that's the poetry of a Congaree preacher on a beautiful Sunday mornin'. Just listen to this ..." And Maxine recited the words as clearly as if she had heard the sermon preached the previous day:

"I vision God standing
On the heights of heaven
Throwing the devil like
A burning torch
Over the gulf
Into the valleys of hell.
His eye the lightning's flash,
His voice the thunder's roll.
Wid one hand He snatched
The sun from its socket,
And the other He clapped across the moon."

When it was certain that Maxine was not interested in becoming another man's wife, her brothers had tried to persuade her to join them where they had both settled with wives outside Cincinnati, but she turned them down flat.

Maxine told Miss Whitecastle one day, "I told those boys, 'Our little sister is buried there in the Congaree with the rest of our family, God rest her soul. You expect me to just up and leave her! I don't think God would be too happy with me over that!'"

Like her father and mother and British immigrants to Charleston before them, Miss Whitecastle was an Episcopalian. She believed in God, but could not *for heaven's sake* understand Maxine's blind faith in the Creator. Once when Maxine was in the car with Miss Whitecastle as they drove to Pawley's Island to open the beach house for the season, Maxine noticed at a stoplight that some power lines covered with vines resembled a massive green cross.

"Look at that Miss Whitecastle, will ya? Jesus is just everywhere I tell ya, everywhere. Just look for Him and he'll reveal Himself. Yes, He will."

Maxine poked her head inside the door again. "All done. Come and take a look," she said.

As usual, Maxine had expertly spaced each blazing pink impatiens in front of the row of rounded boxwoods so that the vibrant colors highlighted the muted green background. Maxine stood with her hands on her full hips, smiling and admiring her work.

"Lovely," said Miss Whitecastle, averting her eyes from Maxine's front side.

For the next few hours, while Miss Whitecastle planned what she would say to the women who would visit her house on Tuesday, Maxine cleaned. Maxine was not her usual chatty self, not once dis-

24

turbing the remainder of Miss Whitecastle's day.

When Maxine had completed all the tasks on Miss Whitecastle's list, she picked up her purse and announced: "Well, I best be goin'. Promised my cousin I'd stop by for dinner."

Miss Whitecastle looked up from her notes. Right away she noticed that at some point during the day, Maxine must have gone to her car and found another, thicker, long-sleeved shirt to change into.

"Maxine," said Miss Whitecastle, handing her a check, "I strongly urge you to seek some medical advice. I don't want to pry, but that … uh … thing … it really looked serious. How long have you had it?

"Now Miss Whitecastle, ma'am," said Maxine. "You don't worry yourself over it. I'll be fine. It's been hidin' under my shirts for a few months now, but I didn't use good sense in what I put on today and now it's got you all in a tither."

"I'm not worried," said Miss Whitecastle tersely. "I just don't think you should ignore it. Can't you ask any of your family members for some financial assistance? Surely …"

"Oh, no ma'am. They've got their own share of worries. I don't want to be worryin' nobody. I'll be fine. Thank you for your concern though. God bless, and you have a mighty fine day."

Maxine let the screened door bang behind her and got into her car. Smiling big, she rolled down the window of her 1985 navy Buick and waved at Miss Whitecastle, who stood propping the screened door open and looking just as distressed as Maxine had found her that morning.

"See ya next week!"

four

During a relaxing lunch that afterward involved sunbathing on a large rock that God had strategically placed directly in the middle of the wide river, Daniel talked about the three's and four's that lay ahead. After a morning of lulling along quietly, the passengers seemed jittery for a little action.

"But what if one of us falls in?" asked Julia. "What is it we're supposed to do?"

"We'll get you back in," Daniel assured her, smiling. "If the rapids pull you along, just lean back on your life preserver. Let your feet and legs float along in front of you. Whatever you do, don't panic. Don't try to stand up."

"Me, panic?" responded Julia.

"You're right," said Daniel. "I frankly have never met anyone so calm and collected."

"Thank you sir," she said. "I'll take that as a complement."

Rose eyed them.

"Don't you agree, Rose?" asked Daniel.

"Whatever," fired Rose, turning away.

Julia shrugged an apology. Daniel hid his irritation at the child's comment by smiling at Julia.

Jon heard Rose and attempted to lighten the mood. "Whatever? Whatever? What kind of citified term is that? Must have learned that one in Charlotte?" he said, laughing.

Rose snickered. She took her seat next to Jon when they returned to the raft.

Everyone piled windbreakers, leftover containers of food, coolers, and the bag of garbage on the floor of the raft. Jon secured some of the items with bungi cords. The passengers put back on their life jackets and situated themselves on the raft's edge, grabbing onto the safety handles. As soon as the raft was fully in motion, the women quickly had an opportunity to test their stamina as the raft began bouncing and spinning over a long stretch of level three waves. Then Daniel shouted commands in short, sharp bursts: "Small waterfall ahead! Left side back paddle! Okay stop! Now everyone paddle forward hard and fast! Hold tight! Here we go!"

Smoothly, the raft tipped forward, fell, and hit the water with a slight jolt. A spray of water covered the passengers. Anxious screams filled the air as the women looked back at what appeared to be a waterfall of significant height.

"Good job," expressed Daniel, slightly amused at his passengers' reaction. He had maneuvered rafts on this river hundreds of times before; knew all the tight spots and how to move around and through them whether the water was low or high. To him, this river was a breeze. It had never offered many surprises – not like the Grand Canyon's Colorado River or the Nolichucky – with the famous "Jaw" class four rapid – that runs through parts of North Carolina and Tennessee. This section of the French Broad was fraught with predictability. He was secretly proud of the fact that he had never even fallen overboard on the French Broad's toughest five's. This was a safe river to bring beginners – with just the right amount of thrills. He was glad to see that the women were having a good time.

"Is that it? Is that the most difficult?" asked Rose. She continued to stare ahead at the river, not making eye contact with Daniel.

"That was just a warm-up," said Daniel. "Niagara Falls is just ahead."

He watched Rose as she allowed for only a slight smile to grace the edges of her mouth. For a split second Daniel permitted his mind to entertain the idea of himself as a father – with a daughter like Rose. He wondered what he would say to her ... do with her?

He was close to 50 and had never been married, or even desired a permanent union. And children. *Forget it.* He shook off the image. *A momentary lack of good judgment*, he decided.

The river slowed again. The passengers absorbed the scenery. Daniel's mind wandered and he questioned why he was interested in spending time with Julia. His general rule of thumb during his entire dating career had been to – if at all possible – avoid women with children. It just complicated the relationship. Got in the way of their fun. But as he aged – even though his fit physique, dark thick hair, and bright amber eyes always passed him for a much younger man – it was more and more difficult to find available women who were not mothers. He could date much younger women, but he hated the thought of being pigeon-holed as one of "those" men. Besides, he liked mature, intelligent, independent women.

Julia impressed him with her keen, natural knowledge of the law, and her gift of working intricate, legal details into a suspenseful smart read. He liked how she was naturally beautiful, not as high maintenance as some of the women with whom he spent time. He respected that she was successful in her own right. He especially loved the fact that she did not take herself too seriously, and was willing to laugh and enjoy their time together. The only instance when he remembered her showing a more serious, withdrawn side was when he inquired about her husband. She had simply answered, "He left," and would not discuss it further. She did tell him, he suddenly recalled, that she was not interested in ever marrying again.

Nothing to worry about then. The child, he decided, was a nuisance he would just have to contend with.

Daniel tightened his grip on the oar and braced as the raft approached another three.

five

Miss Whitecastle did not mention Maxine's growth to her friends in the bridge club on Monday and again at her house on Wednesday for another round of what she considered the highest level of mental stimulation. For Miss Whitecastle, bridge playing was essential – especially after she had retired. It challenged her intellectual capacity as well as kept her tightly entwined in her comfortable social circle.

The women in the club gossiped all right, though they always did it with great concern for their subject matter. But Maxine's name did not come up. Speaking about your servant's ailments was just not a topic to be discussed in such settings. Your own ailments, certainly, or those of loved ones. But not your servant's. This is not to say that Maxine's name never surfaced. The ladies were more than curious about Ellen's loyalty to the aging black woman. They had prodded her on occasion about it. But they resolved that Ellen was somewhat different; they all agreed on that when she was not around. She was the only one of them to actually have had a career – and a career in a man's field at that! She certainly must have her reasons for not hiring someone younger and more capable.

Miss Whitecastle also did not bring up Maxine's name with her brother, Charles, when he visited from Charlotte on Friday. His attitude with her had always been highly authoritative; father-figure like. She rarely shared any information with him about goings on in her life that affected her personally. They kept their relationship on the surface, primarily. She tried to avoid any subject matter that opened the door for him to admonish her.

Besides, it was not necessary to voluntarily bring up Maxine's name because, with predictability, he asked, as he had every time he visited in the five years since he began diminishing his case load and seeing her more regularly, "Are you still employing Maxine to do your cleaning and gardening?"

"Yes," she told him. *You always ask me that and I always give you the same answer and explanation.*

"Why?" Charles asked in his stern, cross-examining style that allowed him some notoriety among Charlotte's legal set.

"Because, she does a good job. I see no reason to let her go," answered Miss Whitecastle, sighing.

"But she's old," he said, ignoring her.

"I don't think she's as old as I am," sputtered Miss Whitecastle.

"Well, the last time I saw her she looked like she was in her 80s at least. Why don't you hire one of those home services that can do it all for you. They're reliable. I told you I would pay for it," he said.

"And I've told you, it's not about the money," said Miss Whitecastle, impatiently.

"What, then?" said her brother. "You know, you don't owe her anything. You have helped keep food on her table for many years. You've gone out of your way to do more than most."

"But I'm her only remaining client, except for Mrs. Hampton who lives in that estate in Shandon," pleaded Miss Whitecastle; she could feel her temples beginning to throb. "She calls Maxine to help with those big parties she sometimes hosts, but that is it."

"Well, it just doesn't make sense to me," said her brother. "Two elderly women trying to take care of this place."

"Is it in shambles?" shot back Miss Whitecastle.

Her brother gave her no answer.

"Well?"

"No," Charles finally said. "It just doesn't make sense to me. What if one of you falls or gets hurt? Neither of you is strong enough to help the other."

"I appreciate your concern," said Miss Whitecastle. "But I don't wish to discuss this further."

"Suit yourself," he said.

The truth was, she did not know why she kept asking Maxine, week after week to come back. Familiarity, she thought. *I'm getting older and just used to the same things.* Miss Whitecastle studied herself for a moment. She could not comprehend why Maxine had been on her mind almost continually since last Saturday. She found her thoughts wandering so badly about Maxine's condition in the grocery store checkout that the college student must have had to ask her several times for her VIP Piggly Wiggly card. *Why else would she have scowled at me?*

And about mid-week she was in such a state after a dream about Maxine collapsing in her yard, blood spurting upwards from the growth on her chest, that she awoke at 3:30 a.m. and was never able to return to her night's sleep. She tried to tell herself over and over again that it was not her concern. Her pesky consciousness would not give her peace, however.

Shortly after their polite lunch of walnut chicken salad and cold cucumber soup at downtown Columbia's Carolina Club, where Miss Whitecastle's CPA license had earned her access, she said goodbye to her brother and began making a checklist for Maxine's arrival the next day. Her blinds had not been dusted in three months, and the baseboards needed wiping.

When the telephone rang that Friday afternoon and she answered it, she immediately recognized Maxine's cheerful voice. "How you doin' today Miss Whitecastle? Mighty pretty day."

"Yes, beautiful," said Miss Whitecastle. "I was just organizing my thoughts for you tomorrow."

"Hate to disappoint you ma'am, but I'm not feelin' so well," said Maxine. "Just wanted to give you a heads-up in case I can't make it tomorrow."

"What's wrong Maxine?"

"Oh, it's nothin' serious I'm sure. Just feelin' so tired ma'am. Might be comin' down with one of those springtime flu bugs or got some allergies to the flowers or somethin'. I think I just need some rest. Maybe I can come one day during the week?"

Normally, Maxine canceling for a Saturday – which, Miss Whitecastle admitted, rarely happened – would have distressed her to no end. However, as Maxine talked, Miss Whitecastle found herself already deep in thought about what her actions would be when she hung up the phone. She could not remember the last time Maxine called in sick. She knew her fatigue had something to do with that growth.

With Miss Whitecastle's pause in the conversation, Maxine said, "I don't mean to throw you off, Miss Whitecastle. You know I'd be there if I could, sure enough."

"Oh … don't worry about it. Just let me know if you can come one day at the beginning of the week. I hope you feel better."

For a few moments after she hung up, Miss Whitecastle sat at the bar in her kitchen, her forehead leaning on her hand. She rubbed at her forehead, thinking.

She picked up the phone again and dialed her internist. Dr. Henry Morgan had been her doctor through a colon cancer scare that ended up being nothing 10 years back. He was also her doctor when she found that lump in her right breast, which turned out to be benign. She was healthy, considering her age. *Walking that dog has kept me healthy. That poodle will not allow for a slow pace!*

"Dr. Morgan's office, please," Miss Whitecastle asked the receptionist. Then, "I'll leave a message."

"Dr. Morgan, this is Ellen Whitecastle. I have a … *friend, acquaintance* … um, someone I know who does not have a local doctor and needs immediate medical attention. Please call me as soon as possible. Thank you."

Miss Whitecastle decided to busy herself to stop thinking of Maxine's dilemma. Who knew when Maxine would be able to clean again? She thought of looking in the phone book for a cleaning service, and then thought better of it. Keeping busy would help derail her thoughts off Maxine. She got out the lemon oil and began dusting, and then carefully polishing, the Charleston-made pedestal table with burl veneers that had been handed down to her by her mother. Had Mr. Whitecastle been alive when Ellen purchased the home 40 years ago, he would have forbade any family inheritance, heirlooms, or mementoes of any kind distributed to his daughter. She regretted, daily, his anger toward her over the cancelled wedding. Even though Joseph is the one who called it off, her father somehow blamed her. *The best laid plans …* She believed her father had been planning the union of his best friend's eldest son to his daughter since she entered the world. Was there ever a time when she had not felt pushed in Joseph's direction, she wondered. Before every social function she recalled her father saying, "Look your best. That nice Barrister boy is certain to be there."

That her father died without forgiving her showed on the furrows that had formed on her brow almost immediately after his passing. Of course, with age, the furrows deepened. Fortunately, wispy bangs always suited her. And even during the fringes of her silver years they blocked the full measure of the lines. Still, they were there as a constant reminder.

The furniture she cleaned was a reminder as well, but of happier times. As a child of Charleston, she enjoyed a privileged, secure upbringing among friends she had known as long as memory served. She and her brother Charles were pretty much left alone to enjoy their friendships; the children they were allowed to play with came only from their own social set. They all lived in similarly styled historic homes made of handmade brick, with a black painted door and brass door knocker, wrought iron fence surrounding the perimeter, creeping fig up one side, at least one – but usually several – Camellia bushes, and rosemary topiaries standing like evergreen soldiers at the entrance. Miss Whitecastle remembered that when it became fashionable for the pineapple motif to be used as interior or exterior decor to convey hospitality, each family in their circle, one by one (*I believe it was the Wentworths who led the way*) chose carved pineapple finials to top the columns of their entryway gates. For their parents, there was the security in knowing that their friends' children were no different than their own children: brought up in the same church, with the same manners, and in familiar dwellings. Thus, they all became almost an extension of one another's family, a sort of clan unto themselves.

One spring day on the piazza, with salty breezes blowing in from the Ashley River, Margaret, Elizabeth, and Janie Anne had all gotten up to the tea table on bended knee, dressed in their full linen dresses, and pretended to drink tea out of Ellen's porcelain set and socialize like their mothers. Ellen wiped over the gouge Janie Anne had made with a knife that she was not suppose to have. She was pretending to cut the cake for their party, slipped forward, and jabbed the knife into the mahogany. *Boy did she get into trouble for that.* Even after a refinishing years ago, the indention still showed in the wood.

When the phone rang, Miss Whitecastle almost dropped the lemon oil. Startled from her thoughts, she raced to the phone.

"Miss Whitecastle, this is Dr. Morgan's nurse,

Mary Joyce. How are you today?"

"I'm fine," said Miss Whitecastle, realizing she was not going to get Dr. Morgan's ear.

"I got your message that you left Dr. Morgan, and unfortunately, he is not taking any new patients. He is at full capacity right now. If it is an emergency, perhaps this person needs to go to a hospital."

"No, it's not an emergency," said Miss Whitecastle, disappointed. "It's just urgent. Is there anyone in your practice who is taking new patients?" she asked.

"I'm afraid not. I checked before calling you. You will just have to try another office. I'm sorry."

"Wonderful," whispered Miss Whitecastle to herself as she placed the phone on the receiver.

In the next moment, she dialed her bridge friend, Annie Francis.

"Hello. This is Ellen …"

"Ellen, what a nice surprise. I did not expect to hear from you until next week. Has our game been changed?"

"Oh … no. I just called to ask you if your husband's practice ever hired that cancer specialist from Atlanta that they were looking at?" asked Miss Whitecastle.

"Oh, Ellen …," gasped Annie Francis.

"No, not for me," said Miss Whitecastle. "For … um … someone I know who needs to be looked at."

"Well, yes dear, he was hired. A Dr. Royal Sanders. Very good I hear. Did a fellowship at Harvard Medical School, Dennis told me. Would you like for me to …"

"Good, thank you Annie Francis," she responded quickly, not allowing her friend time to ask any pertinent questions.

Miss Whitecastle dialed the Columbia Cancer Clinic and asked to make an appointment with Dr. Royal Sanders.

"Are you a patient?" asked the appointment nurse.

"No."

"Who is the referring physician?"

"Dr. Dennis Francis," Miss Whitecastle lied.

"Well we usually hear from the referring physician directly. Is this urgent, Miss Whitecastle?" asked the appointment nurse.

"Yes, very. I would like to see him this coming week if possible."

"Next week? Well, that is most likely impossible. Dr. Sanders is quite booked ..."

"I'm a personal friend of Dr. Dennis Francis, and Dr. Sanders was recommended," said Miss Whitecastle quickly, astonished at the measures she was employing.

"Oh," said the appointment nurse. "Hold just a moment please." For several minutes, Miss Whitecastle listened to Beethoven piped through the phone before the woman returned, "Wednesday at 11 okay, Miss ...?"

"Whitecastle. Ellen Whitecastle. Yes. Fine. Thank you," answered Miss Whitecastle. *What am I doing? Have I lost my mind? What if she won't come with me? Well, if she won't come at least I will know that I tried to help. If she does not want to accept any help, that will have to be her problem.*

Nervous energy prompted Miss Whitecastle to pick up the phone again and dial Maxine. This time when Maxine answered, Miss Whitecastle could detect grogginess in her voice.

"Did I wake you Maxine?" asked Miss Whitecastle.

"Just restin a little ma'am."

"I'm sorry to bother you, Maxine," she said hurriedly, trying to get the words out before she thought better of her scheme, "but if you're feeling better by next Wednesday, I'd like for you to come with me to the nursery to pick out some flowers to plant next weekend. *Why am I lying to her?* I want to try some new varieties this year."

"No problem, ma'am. My clock should be tickin' a little stronger by then. I can come in the mornin' and clean your house that day too if you'd like. Kill both those birds with one stone," said Maxine.

"Only if you're feeling better," said Miss Whitecastle. "See you then."

And before Maxine could question the unusualness of a trip to the nursery for new plants, *I never plant anything new; it's the same year after year*, Miss Whitecastle quickly hung up the telephone.

six

Within a few minutes of passing over another fall, this one made frothy from rocks piled on the river's bottom, Daniel noticed more dark clouds gathering and veiling the tops of the mountains. The air was cooling, and a slight breeze rustled the shoreline trees. A few of the women pulled their windbreakers back on. Julia leaned over to Daniel and quietly expressed concern.

"Probably just a few of those spring rain clouds that quickly pass over," he answered, assuredly. Despite the changing conditions, he was not worried about the weather.

It was nearing mid afternoon. A van from the rafting outfit was scheduled to pick them up at the Hot Springs drop off/pick up site around four. They would make it, Daniel told himself, before those clouds would amount to anything.

But when he turned and looked behind them, the clouds seemed to be thickening quickly into a dark, sooty haze. Ahead of them was still clear and beautiful. He glanced behind him again. Perhaps it was developing into something, he considered.

"Paddle forward everyone," he said suddenly. "We

need to make a little better time. Don't want to be stuck out here after dark," he added with a nervous laugh.

Steady paddling around large river rocks that made something of an obstacle course distracted the passengers from the black curtain that loomed behind them. They had to pay careful attention to keep from bumping into protruding boulders. Once they hit one, sending the raft spinning in a circle.

Daniel noticed an enthusiastic, "Whee!" escape from Rose. *Glad she's at least having a good time.*

Daniel made certain not to alarm his passengers, but for the next 30 or so minutes he was fixated on the sky. When the passengers were not looking at him, he quickly glanced behind him. He studied the direction of the wind; tried to determine the weather's next move. It still looked clear ahead, but behind them the sky was ominous.

Suddenly, the menacing darkness distracted Rose from the river ahead. She pointed it out to her mother and the others.

"It's probably just one of those threatening storms building up," Daniel assured them. "A lot of frightening presentation and then no substance."

The women seemed satisfied with his answer and turned their attention back to paddling. *Why wouldn't they trust me? I told them how long I've been doing this.* But his inner voice was not comforted; he suddenly felt in his gut that this might be a bad one. He looked at Rose, who was staring at him with a worried expression. He felt as if she were reading him, studying his thoughts.

I'll just move them along quickly and look for some sort of shelter, just in case.

Less than a half an hour later a sharp flash of lightning and the immediate explosion of thunder made Daniel realize there would be no time for safety planning. Rose screamed. Julia was the only one who kept her composure and continued to paddle. The other women seemed disoriented and unnerved. Most distractedly set their oars down.

"We'll be okay," said Daniel. "But I need you all to paddle more than ever now. Jon, especially you. You help be my eyes in front of us. We'll find a place to go ashore and get off this river until the storm passes."

He was interrupted by large half-dollar-size drops that began pelting the rafters. Those who did not have them on, scrambled to put on windbreakers. The others pulled their hoods over their heads. Then the rain came in a sheet in front of them, distorting their view of the river. Lighting popped threateningly close. Confusion gripped the frantic passengers. Rose held tight to her mother. Daniel, struggling to maintain control, yelled out, "We'll be fine! As soon as we find a clearing on the shore, we'll pull the raft out. But I need you to paddle. I can't do it alone.

"Make certain your feet are secure in the foot scoops!" To Jon at the bow, he yelled: "I know it's hard to see, Jon, but the first clearing you find, let me know and we'll work our way toward it."

When the passengers collected themselves and picked up their oars, their combined fear and adrenaline enabled them to take the raft hastily through the choppy water. Everyone seemed fixated on finding a clearing, but the shores were dense with trees and boulders. With a jarring impact to the passengers, the raft pitched forward and back over the rapids. Daniel fought to keep the blinding rain from concealing what lay ahead. Whenever he saw anything protruding from the water's surface, he yelled to Jon from the stern. Then he bellowed more directions to his guests. Everyone followed Daniel's short, military-style commands with precision. Every now and then he would convey with confidence: "You're doing great! We're going to be fine!"

"Shore eddy to the right!" yelled Jon. Relief spread across Daniel's face and he abruptly shouted for everyone to angle the raft toward what appeared to be his crew's lifeline. Everyone's eyes were focused on the clearing, which appeared – through the driving rain – to be a slopping, rocky beach ideal for shoring a raft. "Thank God," muttered Daniel under his breath.

But Daniel's keen river sense failed him, for he did not see the boulder to the left until the bow rammed it, pitching the raft high on its side. Everyone scrambled to hold the safety line while gear and coolers spilled into the river. In an instant, the raft scraped along the jagged rock and then came crashing back down into the water. At first glance, it appeared that everyone was accounted for. Daniel's first words were "We have to get control of this raft!" But chaos ensued. Passengers screamed that they lost their oars, shoes, and hats. Even Jon was bewildered. Water sloshed around on the floor of the raft. Daniel, paddling alone, was directing all of his strength and energy into getting the raft back on course toward the shore when he heard Julia scream.

"Rose! Rose is not in the raft!"

seven

Since Maxine was not coming on Saturday, Miss Whitecastle decided – after she filled out her schedule for the upcoming week – that she would clean out the guest bedroom closet that had not been touched in years. Tackling this task, she decided, would keep her mind off of the doctor's appointment she made without Maxine's consent.

Boxes of memorabilia thick with attic dust were brought down by her brother at least six years ago and stored in the closet so that Miss Whitecastle could go through them. Procrastination had ensued and the boxes became a permanent fixture, stacked five deep in the tight closet.

Miss Whitecastle put on a pot of coffee early that morning and situated herself on the guest bedroom floor, carefully combing through her memories. She wanted to distribute some of it to her two nieces, who seemed fascinated with the family's history. *Some of these old things I just need to discard. These things will mean nothing to anyone when I'm gone.*

She pulled out the contents of the closet into the middle of the room and began to make tidy piles on the bed: one for pictures, another for giveaways, a throwaway stack, a re-pack spot. Around mid-morning, she opened the third box and was amazed to find her old porcelain doll, "Annie," at the top of the container. It was her favorite as a young child. Although the lacey dress with the high collar and hand-embroidered details was yellowed with age, the doll's face remained angelic, unaffected by time.

Miss Whitecastle recalled how comforted she was by those blue eyes and blushing cheeks. *What a sweet face*. She carefully laid the doll against the pillow of her guest bed and smiled.

She remembered stubbornly insisting that "Annie" accompany her on vacations and even to their standing dinner reservation every Saturday afternoon at the Ocean Club. "Annie has to go, daddy. If she can't go, I won't go!" He always gave in.

Looking at the doll made Miss Whitecastle realize that Maxine had once mentioned her own favorite childhood doll. During spring cleaning a few years back, Maxine was scrubbing the kitchen floor while Miss Whitecastle sat at the bar, addressing linen paper invitations for a ladies' garden club luncheon she was hosting.

Maxine commenced, "When I was just 10 years old ... Lord, that was a long time ago ... my momma said we was goin' to visit her daddy. Before that, I'd only heard her speak of her daddy one time and it was to call him a 'no good drunk.' Seems he up and left her and her momma when she was little. But all of a sudden, here we are up and goin' to visit him in Santee."

Maxine continued as she worked, "We didn't have a car in those days, so we had to hitch a ride on the cattle car. Well, I said, 'I'm not goin' without

Ruby.' Ruby was my special doll that my brother, David, found on the side of the road and fixed up for me. She was a white doll, and her face always had a crack on it like a scar that didn't heal quite right, but I didn't mind. She was pretty, with a happy smile, and had real lookin' hair. Can you believe someone would just throw a good baby doll on the side of the road?"

Without waiting for Miss Whitecastle to answer, Maxine said, "He cleaned it up pretty, David did, and my momma made a new dress for it, and them two gave that doll to me for my Christmas present when I was eight. Ruby and I were tight from then on. If I was goin' to meet my granddaddy for the first time, then Ruby was goin' with me. I held onto her so tight on that bumpy train. I didn't want her touchin' that smelly floor where them cows or pigs or whatever had been standin' before us.

"Well, we got to Santee and my momma seen my granddaddy waitin' there by the tracks. She just about jumped off that train while it was still movin'. I could tell that all the mad for him must have gone outta her when she seen him standin' there. Soon as the train began to stop, she grabbed my hand so fast and said, 'Come on, Maxine,'" and her jerkin' me like that made me let go of Ruby. She dropped on that nasty floor and momma was just a draggin' me off that train toward granddaddy. I tried to pull away from her and I tried to get her attention, but she just kept on pullin'. All I kept thinkin' was that the train was goin' to start movin again and Ruby was goin' with it. Well, I don't know what came over me, but I planted myself and I screamed louder than I'd ever screamed before. I carried on so that my momma heard me over those loud train noises and she stopped lookin' toward my granddaddy and she looked straight at me. And I can tell you they weren't happy eyes. All I said was, 'Ruby,' and I pointed toward the cattle car.

" 'Lord, child,' she said to me. 'Go and get that doll, and hurry now.' Well my granddaddy just laughed and laughed when he saw all this, and he said I was just like my momma when she was young. He scooped me up and I liked him right on. He and momma must have made up right away 'cause he always came to see us after that, and I never smelled liquor on his breath, not one time."

The remembrance of this scene in the kitchen made Miss Whitecastle think of her own father. He had loved his afternoon scotch, and the odor of it always lingered undiluted on his breath.

The memories quickened as she picked up a silk pouch tied with a tasseled silk rope cord at the top. What had seemed heavy as a child, was not so much so now. The gold coins clinked together as she laid the bag on the bed and unknotted the cord.

It was the last Friday of each month that Miss Whitecastle recalled being allowed to enter his study – a high ceiling, elaborately molded space eerily identical to other professional men's studies up and down Church Street. It was always in the early evening, after he closed up the bank for the week-end, that he summoned her. His scotch was typically larger at the close of each month, a reward for a job well done. The higher the scotch, the larger the num-bers, she used to think to herself.

These last Fridays were particularly upbeat days for the usually stern Whitecastle; the only days, in fact, that her stomach clenched a little less in his presence.

"Come in darlin'," he said. He would drawl out the "darlin'" in the pure Charlestonian manner. She stood by the massive walnut door waiting for his permission to enter. She always felt as if she were stepping into a sacred space. The room loomed large over her. It overwhelmed her with the strong smell of scotch, cigars, leather, and musty hunting trophies.

Books, hundreds of them, filled the floor-to-ceiling shelves encased in decorative fluted moldings. Since she could remember being ignited with a passion to read, she longed to fling open the thick crimson velvet drapes that kept the room dim and make a day of lounging on his button-tufted crocodile hide sofa, drape her feet over one of its arms, and flip through every book. But she had never summoned the courage to even ask. She knew what his response would be. She learned early on his theory regarding women and books: "A dangerous tool for a lady's mind. We can't have America's women filling up their heads with too many facts and figures. Makes their heads too cluttered and their conversations not fit for society. The life of a lady is in her duty to her husband and her family."

His ideals, she often thought, did not seem to fit with the times. When she was a teenager, headlines about a Charleston U.S. District Judge's divorce from his dutiful wife and subsequent marriage to his worldly Northern mistress rocked the city in the early 1940s. The same couple then broke Charleston's ancient Southern code by entertaining blacks in their new home. Barriers were coming down; old rituals fading.

Even her friends thought her father held too tightly to his antiquated views, even though they complained somewhat of a stifling attitude on the part of their own fathers in regard to Charleston traditions.

Painfully, though, Miss Whitecastle learned the consequences of disregarding her father's opinions on matters of correctness. On one of his rare appearances to her bedroom when she was 10 years old, he found her sitting in her cushioned window seat engrossed in Edith Wharton's "The Age of Innocence." It was a book she found sitting on one of the cast iron benches at the Battery one day, waiting for her. Someone had undoubtedly left it behind by mistake, but she could not resist picking it up and taking it home. She immediately became so engrossed in the poetic description of Newland Archer and his secret affection for the exotic Countess Olenska that she vowed to someday read every word of literature that Edith Wharton had ever penned.

"Shameful!" he said, snatching the book from her small hands and staring at the title. "That woman mocks a lady's place ... rebels against it with her words. She has no respect for the roles of men and women in the world!"

She remembers feeling shocked that he even knew the contents of her book. She put her hands to her cheek and recalled the flush of hot anger that rose in her as he ripped large sections of the book and scattered them around the room.

"No daughter of mine will spend even one minute with such ridiculous nonsense. This is what's wrong with our country. Authors like Wharton should never have had a chance to get her disrespectful ideas published!"

She never knew why he had visited her room that day, but she protected her books from then on. She kept them hidden at school or deep in her lingerie drawer, which she knew he would never dare invade. She stole sentences late at night, straining her eyes by her window when the moon was full. Friends at school teased her for always having her "nose in a book" during lunch times and recesses.

Never again did her father catch her reading a book, except for "the" book. Apparently, her elder brother shared her father's opinions about women and books, for he immediately donated Mr. Whitecastle's library to the Charleston Library Association upon his death – despite her ardent pleas to view the books first.

"How's my darlin'?" he always asked her from his leather high back Queen Anne chair perched atop massive mahogany lion's feet.

"Just fine daddy," she would manage.

"You'll be proud of your daddy, sweet rose. Remember that new shipyard coming into our port?"

She didn't, but before she could answer him, he said, "They're getting financing through my bank, sweetie. Your daddy's been wooing them for some time now and they are finally trusting that First Charleston will deliver. Isn't that wonderful, darlin'?"

"That's wonderful, daddy. I'm proud of you," she said, dutifully.

At that, Mr. Whitecastle reached into his pocket and revealed a gold coin. It was a scene that was repeated again and again during her childhood.

"You be a good girl now and put that in your piggy bank."

"Thank you, daddy."

"Now give your daddy a kiss," he always instructed her.

She leaned over and brushed his cheek with her lips. It was the only intimate gesture she was allowed. Her mother had even been instructed to kiss him the same way in public. *Did he show her more tenderness in their bedroom?* She often pondered this as a child, questioning it again now – searching her mind for a glimpse of real warmth between them. Even their family hugs were restricted to a quick squeeze of thanks after the exchange of birthday presents or on Christmas day.

"Formality and tradition in all things," was the motto her father's father had instilled in him, and it was a legacy the Whitecastle family was determined to carry on – despite tradition's slow decay in the rest of American society. Miss Whitecastle looked around her guest bedroom and realized that she had broken from her stately Charleston upbringing in that her taste in furnishings were mostly eclectic, somewhat neo-gothic, with a few pieces of fanciful Victorian she fell in love with at a Columbia antique store, and an ormolu adorned chest that she adored. These were mixed in with the few traditional stately family items that her mother had allowed her. On her walls were some formal oil paintings, but also watercolors by local artists; and, in the master bathroom she even displayed two subtly abstract landscapes she once picked up in Chicago while attending a conference on business accounting.

What if I had told him about his perfect Joseph? What

would that have done to his orderly world? She thought sadly of her father's intense anger and disappointment with her when he learned she would not be marrying Joseph. He would have been equally disappointed, she supposed, if he had known of her decision to study accounting. That she even attended college, instead of getting married, would have been enough. But to study a man's profession. Even though it made no sense – he was already dead at the time she enrolled in the accounting program – she still felt like she did it to spite him. She enjoyed her career as a bookkeeper for a reputable family jewelry business, certainly, but she might rather have spent her days as a librarian, surrounded by books. Even in death, she realized, he had kept her from following her heart.

Miss Whitecastle shook off the memories, placed the coins back in the bag, tied it tightly, and straightened herself. She took the coins and doll into her own bedroom and laid them next to one another on the dresser. She decided enough organizing had been accomplished for the day. *Leave the past in the past is what mother always used to say.*

eight

Daniel whipped around, his eyes immediately searching the river. "Does anyone see her?! Everyone, help me look!" he said. Daniel strained to find Rose, hoping she was clutching a rock close by.

He yelled to Jon, "Get the raft over to that shore eddy. Get everyone onto higher ground. Don't worry about the raft, just get everyone ashore!"

"Daniel, what are you doing? Where is she?!" shrieked Julia, leaning out of the raft as if she were going into the water.

"I'm going to find her!" said Daniel. "Go ashore and wait. I'll find her!" When he saw that she was still struggling out of the raft to get into the water, he yelled again firmly, "Go ashore Julia! I'll find her. You'll do her no good to be out in that water!"

His eye contact assured her enough to sit back down in the raft. He quickly secured his life preserver, made certain his waist pack first aid kit was strapped on, and untied a safety rope.

"Please, please find her," begged Julia, grabbing his arm.

"I will," he said. Then he threw his legs over and jumped into the roaring water. Julia strained to see him, strained to see her daughter, but the rain blinded her.

Within seconds, the raft was safely in the eddy.

"Everyone out!" yelled Jon, without bothering to pull the raft to shore. The water accumulating inside the raft from the rain made it difficult to hold onto against the moving water. As soon as everyone was safely overboard and making their way onto the shore, Jon released the raft. Everyone, except Julia, scrambled, muddy and wet, up an embankment. Julia stood, shaking, at the water's edge, looking down river. She could see nothing but pelting rain on rapids.

"Come on, Julia!" yelled Jon. "We need to hike out of here quickly and get some help!"

• • • • •

When Rose came up for air, she could see nothing but water. Water beating down on her; water splashing in her face. She gulped it, spit it out, and gasped for breaths. She tried to get her bearings, but it was impossible. The raft was nowhere in sight. She concentrated on keeping her feet up. It was the one safety rule she clearly remembered. He explained that a floater with a caught foot could be held under by a current even in shallow water. He said people could drown quickly when their feet became lodged in rocks.

She leaned back on her life jacket with knees and feet up. She tried to backstroke at an angle – toward a shore – but the driving rain and the rapidity of the current disoriented her. Her body struck heavily against rocks causing her to spin or turn over in the water. She fought for breath. A large rock loomed in front of her; she braced herself with her feet. The force of the rock coming in contact with her feet caused her body to jolt, but she clawed at the base of the rock, trying desperately to pull herself out of the water. The swift current took her again and carried her over a small fall. While only about a six-foot drop, she felt as if her body was descending into a cold, watery hell. Her thoughts were of nothing but breathing again. The water from the fall pounded her, turning her over and over again at its base. She felt her body being scraped and battered. But just as the current took her into the fall, it pulled her out of it.

She gasped and cried into nothingness, "Please God. Oh, please help me!" Her body felt limp from the strain of staying afloat, of dodging rocks. The adrenaline that sustained her when she first fell out of the raft was quickly being depleted. Panic and exhaustion began to take over the further down river she drifted.

The impact of Rose's body slamming into a fallen tree caused her breath to leave her momentarily. She desperately grasped the tree's limbs as the water rushing beneath the tree pulled at her legs. Her frantic attempts to inhale only resulted in a moment of hysteria. Her fingers clenched around the tree's branches. Her finger nails dug into the bark. She wrapped her legs around a branch, out of reach of the water's tug.

Slowly her breath entered her again in raspy bursts. When rhythmic breathing was sustained, she calmed herself and began to survey her surroundings.

At first glance, Rose thought she might pull herself along the branches of the tree until she reached the shoreline. With great effort, she struggled through the dense foliage, breaking off whatever limbs she could. Though her legs and arms were strong from a regiment of year-round soccer, they were becoming numb from the cold water and her body ached with the strain on her arms. But she moved, snail-like, along the tree. At its trunk, however, was not salvation but another challenge. A three-foot section of rushing river lay between Rose and the land.

In normal circumstances she might have the courage to attempt the crossing. But her energies were expended and she knew the water would just carry her further down river. She might not survive another turn in the river.

It was best not to risk the crossing, she determined. She would just hold tight to the tree.

The rain beat on her mercilessly. She could no longer feel her legs. Rose began to fade from weariness. Her eyesight blurred as she focused intensely on the river. It seemed the water was slowly rising to where she hung onto the tree. It was touching her backside.

When the morning began, the wildness of the rushing water had secretly thrilled her. Though she had not allowed it to show on her face, she gushed inside with the excitement of a new adventure. Now she felt the river's fury. Its powerful, menacing force paralyzed her with fear.

"This is it," she thought to herself. "This is how it's going to end for me. Mom will find me here cold and stiff ... just hugging this tree."

nine

"Miss Whitecastle, I don't mean to doubt you, ma'am, but I don't think this is the way to the nursery," pointed out Maxine. "And what do you want to get there anyway? Did them ladies at your club get some new ideas of what needs plantin' this year?"

"Maxine," started Miss Whitecastle. "I know of this doctor … a specialist who can …"

"We ain't goin' to no nursery today, are we Miss Whitecastle?"

"Well, uh, no Maxine, we're not. And I apologize for not being forthright with you, but I feel that you at least need to have that growth examined."

"You ever read Job, ma'am?" asked Maxine.

"What?" answered Miss Whitecastle, becoming annoyed. *Why am I bothering with this?* She had almost called Maxine first thing that morning to cancel. All morning while Maxine cleaned her house, she thought about canceling the appointment – and then just telling Maxine that she changed her mind about shopping for flowers. Maxine seemed fine. Perhaps her condition was not that bad after all. Since waking from a restless sleep, Miss Whitecastle had multiple thoughts about the whole business. *It has nothing to do with me!*

"Job. You know, in the Bible?" said Maxine. "Job suffered, but God blessed him in the end for being faithful. God never let nobody suffer for no reason. I figure He put this growth here on me, and He's goin' to use it in some way."

"But Maxine! Don't you think He also gave doctors the gift of healing? For heavens sake, Maxine." Miss Whitecastle checked herself. It was no use revealing her exasperation.

"Well I appreciate your concern, don't get me wrong," said Maxine. "I can tell you right now I'm not happy about it, but I'll go see this so-called specialist since you musta went through some trouble to get this appointment. But I ain't takin' one penny out of your pocket to put toward gettin' me well. You hear me? Miss Whitecastle?"

"Let's just see what he has to say, Maxine."

For the rest of the drive to the doctor's office, the two women sat stiffly, silently, staring straight ahead. Maxine kept her arms folded, looking out the window.

What would people think when she brought Maxine in, wondered Miss Whitecastle. She hoped Maxine would not cause a scene. Practically every time she visited one of her doctors, she witnessed a younger black woman bringing in an elderly white man or woman. She never saw whites assisting blacks. *That's just the way things are. I'll pull them aside and explain that she has been a faithful servant and that I'm just concerned for her wellbeing. That's all it is anyway.*

Miss Whitecastle's urge to flee her current circumstances intensified when she entered the surgeon's formal waiting room with carved mahogany ball and claw foot side tables and gold print jacquard covered accent chairs. After signing in, the two women barely seated themselves before the nurse entered and called out, "Ellen Whitecastle". She rose and approached the nurse. Maxine remained seated. With her back to Maxine, Miss Whitecastle quietly explained to the nurse that the appointment was really for a Maxine Wilkes, but that she wanted charges to be sent to her. Puzzled, the nurse studied Miss Whitecastle, then said, "We can't do that. The appointment was made for Ellen Whitecastle."

She glanced back at Maxine, who was staring at the waiting room television as if she were just biding her time.

"Is Dr. Francis in?" asked Miss Whitecastle.

Bothered, the nurse answered, "Yes, he's in. Why?"

"I'm a friend of his and I would like to speak to him about this matter."

The nurse sighed loudly – loud enough for Maxine to notice. The nurse turned away, mumbling, "I'll get him for you."

Maxine rose from her seat and announced, "This was not a good idea. I just knew it! Now I would like to …"

Miss Whitecastle walked toward her with all the composure she could muster. She looked around. The waiting room was only one-quarter full, but all eyes were on the two women.

"Maxine," said Miss Whitecastle in a whisper. "Everything is fine, I assure you. Please sit down and wait for just a moment."

Before Miss Whitecastle could sit down, another woman – tall and heavy, with down-turned lines around her mouth that gave her a prominent frown – came to the door of the waiting room and called, "Ellen Whitecastle."

"I will be right back," said Miss Whitecastle to Maxine.

Behind the door of the waiting room, the tall woman turned on Miss Whitecastle.

"I'm the office manager. Dr. Francis is with a patient. I understand we made an appointment for you with Dr. Sanders without a physician's referral because you are a friend of Dr. Francis's. But now we have learned that the appointment is really for someone else! I don't quite understand."

Miss Whitecastle could feel her face turning red. She drew in a breath and very politely and quietly explained to the woman that Maxine Wilkes was her servant, could not afford health care, and had a tumor that needed to be evaluated.

"Well, we can see her, but we will have to bill her directly," said the woman, gruffly. "How you assist her financially is your business." She finished with, "Can you imagine how confusing our records would be if we made exceptional arrangements with all of our patients?" She stared at Miss Whitecastle, who did not come up with an answer, before she continued, "We'll call Ms. Wilkes in a moment."

She dismissed Miss Whitecastle by handing her some paperwork, swinging her arm toward the door, turning, and walking away.

Miss Whitecastle handed the paperwork to Maxine. "You just get checked out today and let us see what the doctor says, Maxine, and I will pay the bill." Miss Whitecastle's eyes pleaded with Maxine not to make a scene. Maxine exhaled obnoxiously, pulled a pen from her purse, and concentrated on the paperwork in front of her. The two sat together in the waiting room for what seemed to Miss Whitecastle like a decade. They did not speak. After her paperwork was completed and she turned it in at the reception desk, Maxine sat down and watched the television. Miss Whitecastle eyed the door and watched as nurse after nurse came, called a name, and exited. Finally, a nurse called for Maxine Wilkes. She got up reluctantly and walked dutifully toward the nurse, not acknowledging Miss Whitecastle.

"I'll be happy to go back there with you and …," Miss Whitecastle started, rising slightly from her chair.

Maxine turned. The look on her face made Miss Whitecastle sit slowly back down.

Seated among the traditional Southern décor, she resigned herself to waiting patiently. She picked up an AARP magazine, and attempted to lose herself in an article on the California wine country. She shifted her position in the uncomfortable chair and traced the lines of the sofa's pattern directly opposite her over and over again with her eyes. She put the magazine down, picked up "Carolina Architecture and Design" and half read a piece about a 20,000-square-foot Italian Tuscan-style home on Hilton Head Island. She studied the large floral arrangement on a round centerpiece table in the middle of the room. *Was it real? Certainly not.* She fidgeted in her chair. She was a "case of nerves", Maxine would have told her.

When Maxine re-entered the waiting room at least

an hour later, Miss Whitecastle stood up too quickly. She looked around to determine if anyone noticed her abruptness.

In a high pitched tone of annoyance, Maxine walked toward Miss Whitecastle and said, "I'm ready to go! I didn't want to come here in the first place, and I'm ready to go. I want to …

"Maxine," said Miss Whitecastle in a firm whisper, staring straight into the black woman's large eyes. She coaxed her toward the door as Maxine continued.

"I don't mean no disrespect Miss Whitecastle," continued Maxine as they made their way across the parking lot. She was almost shouting, but in a frantic – on the verge of crying – tone. "I know you means well. But I told you I ain't got the money to pay for these appointments and I don't want no charity either. Lordy mercy. You better let me work that bill off Miss Whitecastle, you hear? I won't be sleepin' at night if you don't."

Miss Whitecastle sighed and did not answer. She knew that bringing Maxine to the specialist had been a mistake. Maxine was upset, angry, and humiliated. Miss Whitecastle wanted to edit the film of her life from the point when she first saw Maxine's tumor to the present moment. She wanted to add in a moment when she feigned complete indifference to Maxine's dilemma and watched the predictability of her week unfold as usual. This was just too much, she decided.

The drive back to Miss Whitecastle's from the doctor's office was sullen and tense. Obviously, the doctor had delivered bad news, but Miss Whitecastle would know nothing of the conversation between the patient and the doctor due to the new Health Information Privacy Act, unless Maxine told her. She decided to cross the line on their relationship, just once more.

"Do you mind telling me what the doctor said, Maxine?" asked Miss Whitecastle politely.

"He said I've probably got me one big cancer growth on my chest," she answered, pointedly. "Said it was more than likely a malignant mass or somethin' or other. Said when that happens, it sometimes gets like roots on a tree that go way down inside a body."

"Yes … and?"

"He said he can biopsy it to be sure, do some surgery, put me on all kinds of medicines, do chemotherapy and maybe radiation, and all that. Might help me to live a tad bit longer. But I ain't comin' back to the doctor for all that. I've not a mind to do that. No ma'am. I've not," said Maxine.

"Maxine, are you sure …"

"That's what I decided before I even seen that doctor, ma'am. I'm just goin' to have to live with it till I ain't livin' no more."

The silence grew between them in large suffocating billows until Miss Whitecastle stumbled on the words, "Did he say … uh … how much longer … until … did he make a determination … about the condition of your … um, health?"

"You mean did he tell me how long I got?" Maxine paused, letting the words "how long" sink in for the first time. "Well I asked him. And he said from just lookin' at it that I probably got me 'bout three months or so. Said I shoulda' come in when I first seen it growin'. He said the cancer's more than likely inside, down deep. Said I'm just goin' to get more and more worn out 'til I can't do much more. Got me one last summer here with the flowers and God's green earth and then I'll be with Him before the chill hits my bones."

Miss Whitecastle drew in a deep breath. She could feel her face flush with the welling of tears. "Oh Maxine, I'm so sorry."

"It's all right ma'am. I knew I wasn't goin' to be here forever. It's all right."

Neither woman spoke the rest of the journey back to Miss Whitecastle's home.

Miss Whitecastle pulled into her driveway, strained with a determination not to cry. She glanced over at Maxine, who seemed deep in thought. Maxine's large dark hands were clasped in her lap and her face was turned toward the window.

She's praying.

Uncomfortably, Miss Whitecastle sat motionless for several moments, not wanting to disturb Maxine.

Slowly, Maxine turned her face toward Miss Whitecastle. Until that moment, she never imagined that a black person's eyes could glow, but Maxine's eyes were brilliant pools of serene darkness. Miss Whitecastle suddenly realized the car was still running.

"See you on Saturday, ma'am," said Maxine as she opened the car door. "We need to get that monkey grass border planted around those pansies, and your hydrangea bed needs some more cleanin' out. And Lord Jesus, if you are havin' another one of those bridge club playins' at your house again soon, I got to get to them windows. I been meanin' to do those windows since Easter time. Your nice ladies don't need to be lookin' through no dirty windows when they're tryin' to concentrate on their hands, now do they? I'll be here at the regular time. You have a good week now!"

ten

   The storm disoriented Daniel, and he was certain
that he had missed Rose. Several times he mounted
a large rock and tried to locate her. He wiped the
rain from his face and strained to see any sign of her.
Nothing. Then he pulled himself to shore and ran
upriver along a rocky beach, searching. He did not
know how far down river he was; he was unsure as
to how long she had been missing. He worried she
was stuck in some crevice between rocks, unable to
move. He dreaded that her body had been carried
much farther down the river than he was looking.
   The water was rising rapidly and the markers
that Daniel always looked for during rafting trips
were being flooded over. His worried state was causing him to lose focus, to forget his river rescue skills.
This was personal, and the river was getting the best
of him.
   Each time he re-entered the river to swim further
down stream, it was with less hope. He knew the
beauty of rivers, but he knew their brutality as well.
Once, when he was camping alongside the Chat-
tooga in South Carolina with a bunch of his old college friends, he helped rescue some high school kids

who were kayaking despite warnings that the river was too high. All six of them wiped out at Devil's Curve, a challenging four during the best conditions, but a nightmare in high water. Three clung to nearby rocks and limbs, while two made it to shore on their own. But the sixth, a 17-year-old girl, was found by Daniel after a frantic three-hour search. Her body was wedged between rocks beneath a waterfall, but he determined that she had probably died not from drowning but from a severe head wound.

This was not the image he wanted to resurface at a time like this. Tightness gripped his organs. He felt nauseated, desperate. He became wild with the fear of finding Julia's daughter too late.

Then he spotted her from a rock a hundred feet away. She was clinging to a tree, her back almost entirely underwater. He let the river wash him to where she was. He tried to grab the tree carefully, but the water caused his body to crash against the tree. The force momentarily jolted Rose's arms lose, but she wrapped them tighter. He maneuvered himself close enough to see that her arms and legs were locked in the branches of the tree. Her body was shaking and her teeth chattering. She glanced his way, but did not make a move to greet him. *She's in shock.*

With one free hand, Daniel rubbed at her arms to stimulate the circulation, while at the same time assuring her that he would get her off the tree and safely on shore. She did not seem to hear him.

Daniel looked around to see how he was going to get her to shore. He knew that she was in no condi-tion – physically or mentally – to swim. He could not ask her to swim. But there were so many branches – as obstacles between them and the shore – that he also knew he could not carry her there.

Daniel spotted a clearing just a few hundred feet down, along the shore. So that his voice would carry above the river's roar and the pelting rain, he yelled his plan to Rose: "I'm going to swim to that clearing ahead! I want you to count to 60 and then just let go of the tree! The water will carry you to where I am and I'll pull you to shore!"

But Rose only stared at him with terrified eyes. She slowly shook her head side to side and began to sob.

"I know you're afraid, Rose, but you can't give up," said Daniel. "You can do this, and you will do this."

But Rose's irrational security in the tree and her new-found fear of the water would not allow her to conceive of letting go. The thought of succumbing again to the river's fierceness was too much to think about. She dug her cold fingers tighter into the wet bark of the tree.

Daniel continued to coax her as his mind raced back to a river safety course he had completed years earlier. He thought first of tying the safety rope around her waist, but quickly dismissed this idea. She could get strangled if the rope somehow wound its way around her neck while she tossed in the rapids.

Daniel knew the longer she was allowed to hold fast to the tree, the more likely a blinding panic would set in. It would be more difficult for her to listen to him rationally. He knew he had to try a different approach, fast.

"Rose, listen to me!" he shouted. "Your arm

muscles are going to collapse soon! You can't stay out here much longer. You need what little strength you have left to get yourself to shore. The river's swelling, and there's a Class 5 waterfall not much farther down river. If more water washes us down, we'll never survive. We have to get you out now!"

He realized he was screaming at her, but it was working. She was looking directly at him, wild eyed and afraid, but listening. So as not to let her think about it too long, Daniel immediately yelled his commands, "When I count to three, I want you to start counting to yourself. When you reach 60, let go. Duck under the tree and lay on your back. Let the current take you down a little ways to the clearing where I'll be. You're a strong girl. You can do it! Okay? One, two, three!"

Daniel let go and in a few seconds he was in a wide sandy clearing, free of fallen trees and debris. He stood waist deep in the tugging water and waited for her. The seconds dragged and he repeated: "Let go Rose. Let go Rose. Let go. Let go. Let go!"

And she did. He watched, nervously, as she slipped underneath the downed tree and let the harsh water thrust her in Daniel's direction. His stomach tightened. Her body seemed lifeless. And then, for an instant, it seemed as if she might not drift close enough. But Daniel strained himself as far out as possible and grabbed at her left hand. He almost lost his footing as he clutched for her right arm. Clumsily, because of the power of the water against them, Daniel pulled Rose to the rocky shore.

Rose was shaking so hard from the cold water that her body was convulsing, as if she were having a seizure. And she was sobbing. Daniel knelt down beside her and pulled her to him. Relief swept over him. He held her tightly. Calmly he whispered to her, "You're okay now" over and over.

After a few moments, Daniel released Rose from his embrace.

The rain pelted them relentlessly. As Daniel helped Rose to her feet, he surveyed the shore to determine if anything provided shelter. A large, uprooted tree made for a narrow, makeshift cave. The dense root system would give them a transitory respite from the downpour.

"Let's get under there for a few moments so I can check to see if you have any injuries," said Daniel. "Then we need to climb to higher ground before this river swells."

eleven

"What is wrong, Ellen?" whispered Mardi Kate, a Charlestonian transplant friend who married into the established Fisher family of prominent Columbia surgeons. Mardi Kate seemed more annoyed than concerned. The two women were in Miss Whitecastle's kitchen preparing a plate of cucumber sandwiches. "You dealt me too many cards, and then you trumped Beth's ace with a diamond. Let me remind you that last month we celebrated your high score. You're committing justifiable homicide, Ellen. Where's your concentration? You seem quite distracted this evening."

"Do you think the others would like a mimosa?" asked Miss Whitecastle.

"Ellen!" said Mardi Kate, firmer this time. "I'm very concerned."

"I'm fine," said Miss Whitecastle, pulling a bottle of champagne and a carton of orange juice out of the refrigerator. If she was going to share her concerns about Maxine with anyone, she guessed it would be Mardi Kate. They had known each other the longest.

"Maxine is ill," said Miss Whitecastle, reluctantly.

"Who?" responded Mardi Kate.

"Maxine, my … um … helper. The black woman who helps me in the house and the gardens. Oh, for goodness sakes, Mardi Kate, she has been in my employ for years now."

"Well, how ill is she?"

"Very ill. She has cancer. She will probably be gone by the end of the summer."

"Well, if you're worried about finding another servant, that won't be a problem," offered Mardi Kate. "I know someone who is absolutely …"

"Mardi Kate! I'm not concerned about finding another … servant," said Miss Whitecastle, taken aback at the high-pitched tone in her own voice.

"What is going on in here, girls?" queried Beth Whitney in her velvety drawl. "It sounds like some friction in the kitchen."

"It's nothing," smiled Miss Whitecastle, grabbing the tray of sandwiches and drinks.

"I'll tell you later," mouthed Mardi Kate to Beth when Miss Whitecastle turned toward the living room where the other women were waiting around the bridge table.

Miss Whitecastle set the refreshments down on the well-set cherry buffet table, polished a rich hue by Maxine. She returned to the game and regained her bridge form. Mardi Kate never forgot an infraction and was often critical, remembering moves months after they had occurred. Some of the women had dropped out and formed their own clubs because of Mardi Kate. Most of the time, Miss Whitecastle let it roll off of her. She was not going to allow her to remember this day on a bad note. When she returned to the table, she paid extra attention to her partner's bidding as well as her lead so that she could return the lead later in the game.

Later that day, after the bridge game and after dozing off in the wicker chaise lounge that occupied her sunroom, Miss Whitecastle awoke to wetness on her cheeks. She sat for several moments, dazed, trying to remember the details of a disturbing dream. While working in the garden, she and Maxine were suddenly seized with panic at an oncoming tsunami that loomed over their heads and came barreling toward them with the force of a train. In the dream, Miss Whitecastle grabbed Maxine and tried to get her to run, but she only stood up, looked boldly at the wave, grinned, and waited for it to overwhelm her. Miss Whitecastle screamed at her to run, but she would not budge. Before the wave struck, Miss Whitecastle ran safely out of harm's way. After the wave receded, she came back to what had become a beach in her vision. She found Maxine, face up on the wet sand, with eyes wide and a dovish expression on her dead face. In her hands she clutched large, broken shells.

Miss Whitecastle touched her cheeks again, realizing that the wetness must be due to tears she shed in her sleep. *Enough!* she scolded herself. *I am entirely too emotional about this whole ordeal. I will not allow myself to become overwrought! I will not!*

twelve

Seldom had Daniel used his slight bit of medical training he learned ages ago when he became a certified raft guide. He was glad he still remembered. He carefully ran his hands over Rose's frigid feet, legs, hands, arms, ribs, and collarbone, checking for broken bones. Her limbs were scraped up fairly badly, as he expected. She would be black and blue with bruises by the next day. He checked her spine. He told her to breath deeply, move her limbs, and tell him if anything hurt. Rose tried not to shiver, taking in deep, gut filling breaths. She could not calm herself completely. It felt as if the cold had taken up permanent residence in her bones. And, anyway, she was alone with this man that her mother supposedly liked; that she was determined not to.

As Daniel's fingers neared Rose's lower back, he felt her muscles tighten. She pulled away in pain.

"Too much pressure?" said Daniel. As she started to speak, his hands found the spot of her discomfort. Her swimsuit was ripped and his fingers met soft tissue. Daniel maneuvered himself behind her to inspect the wound more closely. A three-inch long gash ran perfectly horizontal along the lower right side of Rose's back. Probably from one of the sharp rocks or a branch, thought Daniel. It was bleeding, but the cold water had slowed down the blood flow and had also numbed the area. The pain from the wound would come later.

"What's wrong," said Rose, concerned about Daniel's silence.

"You've got a pretty nasty cut back here," he answered. "It will need stitches, but I'll see what I can do about it now."

From his waterproof waist pack, Daniel pulled out a small first aid kit. Inside was an antiseptic swab and butterfly bandages. He tore the covering off the swab and attempted to clean the wound. Rose felt this. She cringed, tried deep breathing again; tried not to shiver or cry. For whatever reason, she wanted him to know she was brave – not like so many of those wimpy, prissy girls she went to school with.

"Sorry," said Daniel. "Bear with me. I'm going to have to pull the opening together and secure the cut with these bandages. It's going to hurt for a few seconds."

Quickly, Daniel used his index finger and thumb of his right hand to secure the wound while he tightly applied the bandages with his left hand. Six small bandages, the exact amount in the kit, did the job. Then he covered the small bandages with a flat square of gauze and fastened it with medical tape.

"Good as new," he said, forcing a smile. "I think you're going to live," he added.

"Thank you," she managed.

Gathering up his first-aid supplies, Daniel looked out over the swollen river and began to formulate a game plan. He was quiet for several minutes. The rain was still coming down heavily, in wide sheets.

"We need to get to higher ground," Daniel said suddenly. "As fast as this storm came on and as hard as it's been raining for the last hour, we could be in for a flash flood," he told Rose, "and that means we don't need to be anywhere near this river."

Rose remembered camping a few years ago with a friend's church group on the Oconaluftee River in the Cherokee Reservation. A sudden storm had sent them scrambling for higher ground a few miles away. When they tried to return to their campsite, they were told that the bridge leading to the campground had been washed away, as had their camping gear. None of the girls could imagine how water could get that high. They heard the leaders of the group say that a few of the local Indians had stood in the rain during the storm and watched from a cliff above the river. They said that what looked like a wall of water had swooped down on the Oconaluftee and taken with it everything immediately on both sides of the river, as well as bridges perched at least 10 feet above normal water levels. Some of the girls argued that the Indians must have been exaggerating. Rose believed them. She remembered feeling relieved that she had not been one of those on the cliff to watch this horrifying site. She was not interested in another opportunity to view such a scene either. She trusted Daniel to get them away from there.

"Do you think you're okay to walk now," Daniel asked her.

"Yes. I don't really want to stay too close to this river," she said.

Immediately behind their natural shelter was a steep, rock wall. Daniel knew how to free climb but he also knew he could not ask Rose to try it.

She's been through enough, he thought. "Let's walk down this shore a little ways and see if there is a better way up," he told her.

Farther down river Daniel and Rose found an area that sloped up, with large boulders marking a natural, though difficult, staircase up to an overhang. The boulders were slippery from the rain, but both Daniel and Rose were wearing all-terrain hiking sandals, which offered some grip. Rose's battered back hurt with each climb upward, but she told herself she would not complain. At least it was nothing more serious. Whining would only add more stress to their situation. Besides, she was 11. Soon they would find help, she assured herself.

thirteen

"Where did you get them tomatoes?" asked Maxine.

"At the corner stand," answered Miss Whitecastle.

"Tomatoes ain't come in good yet," said Maxine, indignantly. "These can't be good tomatoes. Must of come from Florida or California." She wrinkled her nose in disgust. "If you were thinking about making us a sandwich out of them tomatoes for lunch today, I ain't interested."

It was Saturday. Maxine had been working around Miss Whitecastle's home since 7. Today was baseboard and shutter day. The two women sneezed in unison at the irritating dust stirred up from Maxine's activity. Miss Whitecastle noticed that her employee wore a thick shirt – too warm for the season. Neither woman mentioned anything about the previous week's concern. But Miss Whitecastle still felt weighed down with the thought of Maxine's tumor. She tried, unsuccessfully, to reject her feelings of distress. Why she was experiencing worry with regard to Maxine puzzled her, made sleep erratic, and the last few days scattered.

"Nothing like a good tomato," declared Maxine.

"When you eat one that's warm from the sun and just picked, it's almost better than … well, anything!

"When I was young, 'bout eight I think, my momma told me to go to old Fred Peters' place and ask him for a job pickin' tomatoes in his fields. Would you believe that white man was married to a woman named Wilma? That's a true story. Just like in that cartoon show on TV. Anyway, old Mr. Peters hired me, but my momma didn't warn me that I'd have to be gettin' up at 5 a.m. in the mornin' all summer long. While my friends be sleepin', I'd be workin'. Well, it turned out to be a good thing. Most things momma said were. It weren't hot yet at 5 a.m., and it was all quiet and peaceful like in that field. Made me think about when Jesus would leave his disciples and go out alone to pray. Bet it was that quiet. But the thing I liked most, still do, was the smell of those tomatoes and vines. They smell like nothin' else on earth. Nothin' I've smelled anyway. Sort of peppery and sweet at the same time. It's a smell I can't get enough of, I tell you that. Like to be buried right in the middle of a tomato field.

"After me and some others picked 'til around 9, when it started getting so hot the sweat just poured off you like water from a faucet, old man Peters would load us up in the back of his truck and take us to The Pit Stop down the road. He'd let us pick out two things, a drink and an eat. I always, always got me a Coke and a Hershey's bar. Best breakfast I ever had. Sometimes I still get me a Coke and a Hershey's bar for breakfast … for old times sake. I hope there's tomato fields in heaven, don't you, ma'am."

"I, uh, can't say that I've ever been in a tomato field to tell you the truth, Maxine," she said.

"Oh, ma'am. What a shame. What a shame," said Maxine, shaking her head, before working her way toward Miss Whitecastle's bedrooms with a bucket and cleaning rags in hand.

At 12:30, Miss Whitecastle spooned out some leftover chicken salad over crisp lettuce for herself and Maxine. She poured them both some homemade lemonade and went looking for Maxine. She found Maxine sitting at the edge of her bed with "Annie" in her arms and the bag of gold coins beside her.

"Oh, ma'am, I'm sorry. I saw these things and I just got curious. I'm sorry," said Maxine, flustered. She stood up, "I just never seen these things before. My, what a pretty doll. Did you have a name for her?"

"Annie," said Miss Whitecastle curtly.

"Oh, Miss Whitecastle, I didn't mean to pry," she said apologetically. "You know curiosity killed that cat. Can see why now, can't you?"

"It's okay, Maxine," said Miss Whitecastle, shifting her composure. Then, moving toward her, she picked up the bag of gold coins. "My father gave me these. Would you like one?"

"Oh no ma'am, I couldn't. Never had seen a gold coin in person before though. This is like a bag of real treasure."

"Just a bag of memories, Maxine."

"Well, it's nice to have them all wrapped up and tied with a fancy string like that," said Maxine, smiling.

Miss Whitecastle's face warmed. "I suppose you're right. Now let's have some lunch. I want to get those flower beds in good shape before you leave."

After lunch, Miss Whitecastle watched as Maxine carefully cleaned beneath the massive hydrangea bush that gifted the yard with powdery blue blooms each season. Then she emptied bag after bag of pine bark mulch under the sprawling bush, and around the patch of red rose bushes, stopping often to take a sip of tea, straighten her back, and wipe perspiration from her face with the inside of her shirt collar. It was Miss Whitecastle's assignment, according to Maxine, to cut the bags and supervise the efforts.

When she finished that task, Maxine exclaimed, "Where's my mind! I almost forgot to vacuum the dining room."

"Maxine, you've done enough for today," said Miss Whitecastle. "Don't worry about that today. You go home and rest now."

Surprised, Maxine said, "Now, Miss Whitecastle, when have you ever known me not to finish my job? It'll only take a minute."

When Miss Whitecastle heard the high-pitched whine coming from the vacuum cleaner, and then silence, she knew what would happen next. The same scene unfolded when hedge trimmers suddenly stopped working last year, and when the dishwasher ceased to clean the dishes five years earlier. Without hesitation, and muttering "lordy mercies" under her breath, Maxine marched past Miss Whitecastle and toward her car. Predictably, she pulled a large toolbox out of her trunk. Without a word, she disappeared back into the house.

Miss Whitecastle knew not to intervene. She made the mistake of questioning Maxine's mechanical abilities only once. Maxine possessed a manly ability to decipher the complexities of anything with moving parts. Only once did a malfunctioning hot water heater prove too much for Maxine's innate talents.

Within a few moments, Miss Whitecastle heard the toolbox lid click shut, and then the whir of the vacuum as Maxine finished the dining room.

"Ain't it about that time of the year to fix up your beach house, ma'am?" said Maxine, strutting proudly by Miss Whitecastle with the vacuum in hand.

Miss Whitecastle had completely forgotten about her annual Pawley's Island ritual. *I've been way too preoccupied lately.* Opening the home in late spring required that both she and Maxine make the two hour drive, uncover all the furnishings, fold and store the sheets, dust the furnishings and vacuum. After a day of driving and cleaning, Miss White-castle always ordered a seafood meal for the two of them from Shabby's. Then they would retire to bed early and return to the state's capitol first thing the next morning. A week or so later, Miss Whitecastle would begin a series of excursions to her Pawley's home that would last well into the late days of summer. This was a ritual she had begun since retiring almost 15 years earlier. Sometimes she brought friends, and always – on at least one trip – her nieces and their children would accompany her.

In late August, and occasionally in early September, Maxine would again make the drive with Miss Whitecastle for the house closing.

"It is about that time," answered Miss Whitecastle. "Are you up for it this year Maxine?"

"Why, I feels as though I am right now. I plannin' on it. I sure do love the beach." Then, she added, "This might just be the last time I see that great blue ocean."

"Oh Maxine," lamented Miss Whitecastle.

"Now Miss Whitecastle, it's okay. I can't tip toe around it. It's happenin', ain't it. Besides, I'll see things much sweeter in heaven than that blue ocean, I'm sure of it."

Miss Whitecastle sighed, gathered up the empty mulch bags for the trash, and announced to Maxine, "That's enough for today."

Inside, she closed her bedroom door behind her, found a washcloth in her master bathroom, wet it, and held the chilly wetness to her face. She had again felt herself become flush when Maxine mentioned dying. After regaining her composure, she dried her face. Walking back through her bedroom, she spotted the doll and coins. In the corner, among some unopened cardboard boxes that she had transferred from the guest bedroom to her bedroom, she spotted a small wooden box with mother-of-pearl inlay. *The box of letters. How did I miss that?* Stricken, she wondered how she had not noticed it before. In her distracted state, she realized she must have mindlessly carried the box into the room with the other items. Had Maxine snooped inside the box as well? She suddenly became angry. A spasm of irritation crossed her face and her shoulders tightened.

She sat down on the bed, placed the box in her lap, and slowly opened the lid. It had been at least 10 years since she had visited this part of her life. As she did now, she had often wondered why she kept the letters. She knew that if someone were to stumble upon them and read them, she would not be able to explain them away.

Did Maxine read them? They did not appear to have been opened in a long time. She pulled the top one off the stack and the envelope flap was stiff and crackly. She dared to pull the letter out of the envelope and began to read. The contents stabbed at her heart. Guilt wrenched her stomach. She picked up another and opened it. This one from her brother. *It's too late now.*

She neatly folded the letters, returned them to their box, and crammed the box in the dark recesses of her closet. *Why do I do this to myself?* She made up her mind that she would destroy the box, burn it in her fireplace, but not today.

Miss Whitecastle sat on her bed for what seemed like hours. She tried not to remember. Tried not to feel regret and shame. But it was always with her – sometimes a small seed, while at other times an obnoxious thick vine strangling her from living a burdenless life.

"You in there, ma'm? You okay?" Maxine was on the other side of the door.

Her suspicion about Maxine reading the letters exited her mind. She convinced herself the letters had not been opened; Maxine had not had enough time to read them anyway. She decided she would not question her about them. *It will only make her wonder why I'm concerned. She'll pester me about it.*

"Ma'm. You makin' me worry now. You okay?"

"I'm fine. Be right out Maxine."

As she was rising from the bed, she glanced again at the doll and the coins. In a sudden burst of spontaneity that she could not remember experiencing, except for a few rare moments during her youth, she picked up the doll, lay it gently in an empty shoebox situated at the top of her to-go pile, and plunked in two of the gold coins from the bag. She felt a sudden boost as she left her bedroom.

Maxine stood at the screened doorway waiting patiently for payment from her employer. After handing her a check, Miss Whitecastle thrust the box at Maxine abruptly.

"I want you to have this," she said, nervously. "I was just going to get rid of it anyway. It has been sitting in my closet for years. It will be more at home with you."

"What's this? Oh ... Miss Whitecastle. What's this ma'am. Oh ... no, I can't take your doll ma'am. This is the prettiest thing I ever seen. I can't take this from you. No ma'am."

"Maxine, I insist. Please. It will just find its way into another box heaped in the back of a closet somewhere. You can enjoy it for ... a time."

A cumbersome moment of silence ensued between them.

"Thank you ... ma'am," said Maxine, shyly. She turned and walked toward the car, both arms clutching the box to her chest.

fourteen

As the attorney/rafting guide and injured child picked their way up the jagged rocks, slimy with wet moss, the French Broad River swelled below. Daniel was behind, coaxing Rose over and around the obstacles. He winced at the blood stain that formed on her swimsuit from the wound he had treated. He knew she must be in pain with every movement up the embankment, but she offered no complaints. This was not what he expected of a child.

When they were 20 feet or so above the river, something made Daniel look back. What he saw confirmed his worst fear. Where he earlier pulled Rose to safety was now underwater. Soon the river would be spilling onto the banks and into the valleys, causing flash floods.

But the thought he shuttered at came just minutes after he and Rose reached the top of the 40-foot cliff. The river was now one and a half times the size it was only hours before. Water that had been mildly turbulent now exploded with the rampage of the storm that ensued.

Daniel placed his hand on Rose's shoulder, guiding her to a safe distance from the cliff's edge. A wall of water, at least six feet in height, roared down the river with the power of a freight train. The mountain's version of a tidal wave.

He had never seen it before in person, but he watched with Rose in awe and horror as trees along the shore were ripped up from their roots by the sudden impact of giant rapids making contact. The water seemed to take on a life of its own, gathering whatever debris it could carry with it downstream to a watery abyss.

Rose began to cry. Daniel put his hand on her shoulder and turned her away from the river. "My mom," Rose struggled between sobs. "What if she's not far enough …"

"She is by now," said Daniel, convincingly. "Jon hasn't been doing this that long, but he has already learned about flash floods. He would have gotten them far away from the shore by now. They're probably with the rangers right now, dry, safe, and waiting for a rescue team to find us. Don't worry."

Daniel squeezed her shoulder, mustering compassion.

He had plenty of experience comforting teary-eyed women, but a child was different. He considered himself void of fatherly instincts. He did not even own a pet. His own father had supported him, kept him clothed and fed, and even encouraged him with good advice. But never did he show him affection. His mother, on the other hand, showered him. She was kind, but overwhelming in her attention toward him. He often felt smothered and emotionally overwrought by her demonstrative nature.

He felt certain it was his mother's yearning to mother that had pushed his father down the adoption road. His father, though not an abusive man, never gave him the impression that he much enjoyed being a father. And they had not adopted more children.

He wanted to question his father, but was afraid. In adulthood, though, Daniel was beginning to gather enough nerve to ask him: Did you really want me? But, and he blamed God for this, the church they were helping to build in Peru with a mission group crumbled during an earthquake. His parents died and left him even more curious about their intentions.

Daniel realized Rose had stopped crying. "Let's go," he said, leading her down what looked like a crude path.

For several minutes, Rose and Daniel walked in silence. What they had just experienced had unnerved them both, though Rose more.

"Do you think … that they'll be okay? Do you think … that they'll be safe if we pray for them?" asked Rose, hesitantly. "Do you think God really listens to us? Do you think it will help?"

Daniel suddenly felt the same tension rising up the neck muscles connecting the base of his skull that he experienced when a client's questioning annoyed him.

"Yes, I think they will be okay. There are several roads on that side of the river that lead to homes. I have no idea if praying will help or if God listens," he answered her, brusquely. "But if you would like to pray, you go right ahead."

With that, Rose was silent. Daniel hoped he had closed that door; closed it shut. He had no interest in talking about God and religion. He saw no evidence of the higher power in his life. Never had, never expected to. His success, he decided long ago, was based on his own ambitions – not on some unseen spirit.

Daniel studied the small compass he had attached to his safety pack. He had some idea where he was leading them, but had never really explored this side of the river. The landscape changed back and forth from thick, almost impassable masses of twisted briars and interlocking chains of rhododendron to sparse areas of evergreens and hardwoods, bedded with ages of thick leaves. The Western side of the French Broad was dense with tight mountain laurel groves and multi flora rose thickets. Massive rock formations protruded from the earth like jagged skyscrapers. Some formed dark, cave-like entrances. Very little light from the gray sky above penetrated the thick forest.

The rain was beginning to subside somewhat. Instead of a deluge, it had turned into a steady shower. The silence between them was awkward, but Rose decided to use the time to pray and see what happened. The forest was quiet, eerily quiet. She wanted to hear the voices of other people. She wanted to see a building or a campground, something. She wanted to know her mother was okay.

Daniel checked his watch. It was getting late in the afternoon, closing in on early evening. The tangle of evergreen foliage was not clearing onto any dirt roads or even distinct paths. He did not want to be out here with her after dark. The longer they were missing, the more panicked Julia would become. Sometimes Charlotte broadcast the news of the Asheville area if teenagers or college students went missing for several days in the mountains. Always when the parents were interviewed, their frantic, sleep deprived faces expressed the anguish of not knowing. Had their child died of exposure? Was it a hungry mountain lion? Did they fall off of a cliff? Daniel remembered the story of one lone hiker who had somehow gotten stuck in a tree during the spring, perhaps to get a better view of his surroundings, and his skeletal remains were not found until the winter, when the trees were bare. He hoped that Julia's imagination would not run wild. *It will if we're stuck out here for the night.*

Had it been any other time, Daniel would have enjoyed the solitude and ruggedness of this wilderness. The mountains afforded him a pleasant release from the harshness of family law, with all its injustices and mean-spirited squabbling over money, objects, and children. The rain had enlivened the mint fragrance of the birch. Everywhere was lush, saturated foliage in rich tones from light to dark green. It was trillium season, and the white blooms hung gracefully from their long stems in patches along the trail.

The senior partner at the law firm where he had been employed since finishing law school and acing the bar was one of the few people he knew who grasped Daniel's ardor for this region. *Why else would he have given me unlimited access to his mountain lodge?* They often discussed their mutual longing for the mountains after weekly firm meetings or over lunch.

Daniel realized Rose was slowing down. He knew she was in pain from her wound; that her tired legs must ache with every step. His own body felt heavy from his wet clothes and from weariness. He was feeling every bit of his 50 years.

"We should be coming to a real road or a path here sometime soon," said Daniel encouragingly. "I've not explored this side of the French Broad before," he added, "but there has to be some signs of life nearby."

Daniel checked his compass again. "Let's head over this way," he told her, turning toward a small hill that looked as if it were covered with more large patches of rhododendron.

Rose sighed with exhaustion, but mustered up a bit more energy to follow him. They ducked under and climbed through a wall of the scraggly plants, which inflicted both of them with scratches. Finally the interwoven bushes thinned out and their view became clearer. Ahead of Rose and Daniel was a road, archaic and fraught with ruts and holes, but a road. Daniel gave Rose a look of relief.

The rough road was narrow, and Daniel wondered if a car could have driven on it. *Something had to keep this clear.* He was certain the road would lead to a home soon. They would call for help, and in a few hours this would all seem like an unpleasant dream.

fifteen

Tucked warmly beneath a down comforter and 400-thread-count sheets, Miss Whitecastle's aging limbs jerked upward at the sudden high-pitched whirring of A. T.'s old riding lawn mower. *What time is it?* She breathed deeply, relaxing again – somewhat – before she strained to see the time on her clock. *Nine o'clock. My goodness, gracious!*

After a few weeks of what seemed like constant restlessness, sleep had finally blessed her taxed frame. The exchange with Maxine the previous Saturday gave her a jolt of hopefulness. Miss Whitecastle admitted to herself later that evening that it had been her generosity toward Maxine that brought about the change in her own countenance. It eased a nagging inner penitence. She felt a greater peace. She had not sensed such a closeness with Maxine since the incident 20 years earlier when a drug addict had robbed Miss Whitecastle of her purse and car. When she came home from work one evening, she parked her car in the carport as usual, unlocked the entryway door and set her purse down inside. Then she walked to the side yard to let her dog out. When she was returning to the front yard with the dog, her car was backing out of the driveway. In that short amount of time, the thief escaped with her purse and her car.

The following week, Miss Whitecastle experienced the depths of Maxine's compassion. Homemade soups, yeast breads, and always a gallon of tea, graced her porch each afternoon when she arrived home from work. Reliably, a note accompanied the feast. "Now don't forget to turn on those outside lights." "Keep them inside lights on too." "Make sure that dog's in there with you at night."

"Thank the Lord, oh thank the Lord," said Maxine, when she had arrived at 7 a.m. that next Saturday after the theft. "You could have walked up on that boy and he would have broken your bones. Sure enough, some bones would have been broken. Oh, Miss Whitecastle, you must a been scart to death! When them boys is on drugs, they don't know what they doin'. They will steal you for a nickel … for nothin'. They just ain't thinkin' when them drugs gets hold of them. Thank the Lord for protecting you!"

Thoughts of Maxine suddenly brought to the surface a dream Miss Whitecastle realized she must have been having when the lawnmower woke her. She lounged against her feather pillows, eyes closed, recalling the dream. Again the scene was beach-like, with a giant wave that overtook Maxine. This time Maxine fully embraced the wave and rode it, thrillingly and youthfully out to sea. As Miss Whitecastle stood helplessly on the shore, foam swirled around her feet. When the foam dissipated, shells covered her feet.

Her eyes opened and she was struck with a sudden effervescence. She showered, dressed, drank a cup of coffee, ate a cranberry orange muffin, and picked up the telephone.

"Maxine," said Miss Whitecastle.

"Miss Whitecastle. Well how you today ma'am? Got some silver that needs polishin' this comin' Saturday?"

"I'm fine Maxine, thank you. No. The reason I'm calling is that ... well ... I would like to know if you will be able to accompany me to Pawley's Island this Saturday?"

"Well, yes ma'am, I think that will be fine."

"But this year Maxine, and I don't want you to say anything until I'm finished ... but I want you to stay there with me for a while."

"Ma'am?"

"I would like for you to be there and ... um ... just enjoy the beach this summer."

Maxine was quiet. Miss Whitecastle heard her clear her throat.

"Ma'am, now don't get me wrong. I 'ppreciate it. I do," said Maxine. "But I ain't got the money to be traipsin to the beach. I got to keep workin' ma'am."

Miss Whitecastle held the phone in her hand. She stood silently for a moment. She knew this was not going to be easy. Desperation arose in her.

In a low, almost pleading voice she spoke slowly, "Maxine, I want to do this. I ..."

"Ma'am, you are so kind. But you don't owe me nothin'. Just payin' me for workin' all these years and keepin' me on when I'm gettin' older has been enough I tell ya. Enough. Shore is, ma'am. Now I'll go with you like I always do to Pawley's, but you don't need to go frettin' yourself over me havin' some last days on the beaches. I do 'ppreciate it though."

Miss Whitecastle could feel an ache rise again in her temple. *Why is this so important? Just let it go.*

"Maxine, I ... ahhh!" gasped Miss Whitecastle, dropping the phone. It hit the linoleum and bounced a few times before lying still. In front of her stood the very tall and perspiring A. T. in the doorway to her kitchen.

"I'm so sorry ma'am. I rang the doorbell and knocked, but no one answered. I knew you were here by your car in the driveway. Sorry to frighten you ma'am. I thought something might be wrong. Door was unlocked."

"It's ... okay ... A. T.," she said, picking up the phone. "Maxine ..."

"Lordy mercy, Miss Whitecastle. What's happenin'? Are you okay?"

"I'm fine. A. T. just startled me, that's all. I will call you right back."

"Ma'am, I'm really sorry," said A. T. "Guess you were okay before I came in here. I rightly could have given you a heart attack," he apologized.

"It's okay," said Miss Whitecastle, writing him a check. She handed it to him and, still distracted, turned her back to him dismissively while he remained standing in her doorway. It was not until the screened door closed behind him that she realized she had not thanked him. Opening the door, she called, "Thank you A. T. Just check on the grass next week. If I'm not here, I'm at the beach. Call me and I'll send you a check."

Her headache was in full force, with a burning sensation between her eyes. The muscles at the base of her skull felt tight. She sat at the end of a sofa in her living room and began to massage her temples. She did not want to call Maxine back, did not want the awkwardness of another bungled conversation between them. The phone rang. It was Maxine.

"I'll go ma'am," she said.

"You ... will?"

"Yes. I'll go because I started thinking that I been workin' all my life and I think I just want to stop and smell the roses ... or, I guess smell the sea, before I'm leavin'. I don't want to be smellin' the Lysol on my last day." At this, she laughed out in one loud burst.

Miss Whitecastle smiled.

"I just don't want you spendin' any of your money on me that don't have to be spent. I'll help you out doin' stuff there and earnin' my keep. You hear?"

"Perfectly. See you on Saturday Maxine."

sixteen

Darkness was settling on the mountains and there were still no signs of civilization. Daniel was visibly discouraged. Rose's pain from the gash on her back was unbearable. Her legs were concrete blocks. The cold from the rain settled into her joints.

"Mr. Daniel, I don't mean to complain," she finally said, "but I'm not sure I can keep walking."

"I know," he answered. "I've been looking for a place to take shelter for the night. I'm sorry, Rose," he said, meaning it. "I thought this road led to somewhere."

As he was talking to her, something caught his eye. "What's that up ahead?" he asked, mostly to himself. He strained. She saw it too. A faint light twinkled through the trees.

Without another word, Daniel started walking toward the light. Rose mustered a sudden burst of energy and followed quickly behind him. It was difficult to determine from where the light source emanated. As they sloshed along on the muddy road, the light in front of them became a beacon.

I knew we'd find a home.

What they began to make out through the dusk

was a shelter of some sort. As they closed in on the habitat, they could see that it was actually a dilapidated, old cabin, with a main front section and then a sprawl of small additions haphazardly attached to one another. The main part of the house was made of rough hewn boards, but the rest of the spaces included bits of wood and tin, arbitrarily hammered together to create a homely dwelling. The light was illuminating through one of the few windows in the structure.

The surroundings were a treasure trove for a junk collector: old tools, scraps of tin, pieces of a car, and even the springs of a bed. This and much more littered the makeshift yard. A small, muddy pen held a few pigs, and another pieced together enclosure was a chicken coop.

"It's hard to believe someone actually lives here," whispered Rose.

"I don't care how they live," said Daniel. "I just hope they will be friendly and helpful. And I hope they have a phone."

Rose and Daniel approached what they assumed was the front door of the establishment. As soon as they knocked, a great burst of howling and barking came from inside the house. They could hear a scuffle, and then a voice boomed, "Who's out there?"

"We're rafters who got caught in the storm!" yelled Daniel over the commotion. "Do you have a phone?"

"No!" boomed the voice again.

"Can you take us into town?" Daniel tried.

"No!"

"Sir, I have a little girl here who is injured and she needs some help!" Daniel said in desperation.

The inhabitant did not reply.

"Sir!" yelled Daniel, exasperated.

After a few moments of dogs barking and no word from the person inside, the door creaked open. Rose could see a gaunt woman shuffling to keep two hound dogs from bursting through the crack in the door, while the robust man of the house greeted them with a shotgun in his hand.

"Listen," roared the owner, his veins visible at his temple; hair disheveled and oily. He pointed his gun their way in a gesture of intimidation. Standing square in the doorway he said, "We live out here for a reason. We don't want no strangers on our property. Sorry for your trouble, but we want you gone, and that means now!"

"She's injured," said Daniel bristling, nodding toward Rose. "Surely you have some way of communicating with people ... a phone, maybe?"

"You see any phone wires 'round here? We ain't got no phone. Now go!"

Daniel was insistent. He did not give up easy in the court room and he was not going to back down now, gun or no gun. His weariness and frustration made him bold, even in the presence of a double barrel at eye level.

"We at least just need a place to rest until morning," he pleaded.

"Now!" repeated the man, tilting the gun barrel toward Daniel's face and putting his pointer finger directly onto the trigger.

Daniel's anger and impatience was beginning to overtake him. Rose could sense that. She stepped toward Daniel and tugged at his arm. She begged him, "Please, let's go."

The man slammed the rickety wooden door in their faces. The dogs continued their howling. Rose and Daniel stood dumbfounded for a few moments. They could hear arguing from inside the house.

"Bastard!" said Daniel under his breath. He looked at Rose. He knew she had heard him. He did not apologize.

It was almost dark now. Daniel found the road again and the two began walking down it – silently. Rose shivered from the dampness and from the stress of what had just occurred. Rain continued to drench them. She was searching for words to encourage Daniel, just like she did with her mom when rejection after rejection arrived in their mail box or by e-mail. "Your novel is great mom. Someone will publish it," she told her many times. Then her mom had hit it big. "See mom." Adults needed encouragement sometimes too, she thought.

But it was Daniel who broke the dead air with wrathful words: "A lot of good your prayers did us."

Rose did not respond. She was listening for an approaching sound.

Daniel heard it too – footsteps coming up behind them. They turned. Rose could make out a person and could see the outline of the shotgun. Daniel instinctively grabbed her and pulled her behind him.

"We're leaving!" said Daniel with contempt. "We don't want any trouble!"

As the figure neared, they realized it was the man's wife.

"My husband doesn't take too kindly to people. They've done him wrong. We've got an old barn in the back with some hay in it. You can stay there for the night, but you better be outta here at sunrise."

"Thank you … ma'am," said Daniel, hesitantly. The woman turned away and began marching back up the road toward her home. Daniel and Rose followed her.

seventeen

The crushed oyster shells crackled under the hot tires as Miss Whitecastle pulled the car into the driveway of her beach cottage. Hers was actually one of the only long driveways on the island. The quaint cottage, nestled among gnarled live oaks heavy with Spanish moss on one side and a short narrow boardwalk to the beach on the other, was purchased by her daddy from one of his bank clients – a descendant of one of the old rice plantation owners who once thrived on Pawleys.

The cottage was named after one of the families that settled in the area, the Landers. They were one of several South Carolina planters who took advantage of the tidal wetlands for the cultivation of rice. Miss Whitecastle remembered reading that by 1860, a few of those wealthy Georgetown County planters were credited with producing more rice than any other area of the world – except for Calcutta, India. These planters typically owned town homes in Charleston, mountain homes in Flat Rock, North Carolina, and then began building homes on the four-mile stretch of Pawley's Island to escape the mosquitoes and malaria of the inland towns.

But after slaves were no longer available to work the labor-intense crops, rice cultivation eventually failed. Those first beach cottages, made of pecky cypress and rough-cut cedar, suffered from neglect, but remained protected by the barriers of naturally high dunes. Once South Carolinians got back on their feet, the coast became a desirable getaway again and more houses crowded around those original dwellings.

Miss Whitecastle's brother was the natural heir to the cottage, as he was to the 4,000-square-foot hunting cabin outside Asheville that he liked to call "cozy." Her daddy would never have left either of the two desirable properties to her, considering what she had done. Even her mother, who in her quiet way had eventually forgiven her daughter for shaming the family name, would not have approved of her owning such expensive family real estate. But her brother thought differently. Besides, for reasons she never quite understood, he detested the coast as an adult. After a respectable amount of time spent grieving for their mother, Charles presented his sister with the Pawleys Island cottage as an unexpected gift.

"You can have your sea," he had told her, "while I'll take my mountains."

Miss Whitecastle remembered her childhood summers at the cottage as freedom from the pretenses of Charleston and the strict demands of her father. He stayed behind to manage the bank, only joining them on some weekends. A local Gullah man, Philemon, delivered their ice in giant blocks for the icebox; an ice pick hung nearby so they could chip off chunks of ice for their lemonades and teas.

Sometimes Philemon brought them fresh catches of shrimp, crab, and flounder. She and her brother journeyed to the little store next to the post office for dairy milk, with a layer of cream on the top, in glass bottles. Sometimes they purchased a sucker bar or an ice cream at the Pavilion and returned to their rope hammock to lounge and allow the sweetness to melt and stick to their face and fingers.

With her husband gone, Mrs. Whitecastle loosened her grip on her children. She also wore her hair less securely. And, on occasion, the children caught her walking around the house without shoes. Late some nights, when they were suppose to already be sleeping, they heard the front door open and close. Charles snuck out and followed her one time, reporting to his sister later that their mother was walking barefoot on the beach in the moonlight.

They were permitted to spend most of their days in their swimming clothes. But when her father sent word that he would be visiting for a weekend, the mood inside the beach cottage would change. The lightheartedness they enjoyed in his absence dissipated, replaced with a regiment of social obligations while he was present. Other Charleston friends vacationing on the island were invited for drinks and dinner, while Ellen and her brother Charles were expected to dress appropriately and excel at their manners regarding hospitality. Her father would bring Lula, the family's cook, with him on his weekend visits. Lula was famous with the Island set for her cheese grits and shrimp, and for preparing deviled crab with just the right amount of Vidalia onion. Guests of Mr. Whitecastle looked forward to Lula's lavish spreads.

Maxine grabbed her one bag out of Miss White-castle's car and stood beside the cottage's brick foundation – made by slaves' hands – waiting for Miss Whitecastle. Behind the house, partially covered in a wild red rose bush, were the remains of a slave cabin. Maxine watched as the gleaming ebony grackles landed on a wax myrtle nearby, announcing their arrival with their obnoxious "sheek, sheek sheek". A weathered black man holding his fishing pole rode by the entrance to the driveway on his bicycle, paying no attention to Maxine.

"I can put this bag down upstairs and help you some," said Maxine.

"Don't think of it," said Miss Whitecastle. "You're here to rest."

"Thank you ma'am, but I've got eternity to rest," said Maxine. "I may be sick, but I ain't dead yet."

Maxine labored up the stairs to the back entrance, propped the screened door open with her bag, and then returned to the car to collect the pillows and sheets. Another trip up the stairs and Maxine collapsed onto the kitchen chair as soon as Miss Whitecastle unlocked the back door.

"Maxine!" said Miss Whitecastle, alarmed.

"Oh, I'm all right. Don't worry yourself none. Just gotta catch my breath, then I'll help you out around here."

"There will be none of that," said Miss Whitecastle.

As Maxine's breathing slowed, she looked around and realized that the furniture had already been uncovered from the thin white sheets that protected it throughout the winter. The air conditioning was humming, and the house smelled like orange Lysol.

"I found a service that would come in and prepare the house this year," said Miss Whitecastle proudly. "There is no need for us to lift a finger this time. There is even someone who will deliver groceries. Like I said before, you are here to rest."

"You mean to die, ma'am," said Maxine.

"Maxine!" gasped Miss Whitecastle. "Must you be so morbid?"

"Sorry, ma'am, but it's the truth, ma'am," answered Maxine. "I can't fool myself into thinkin' I might be leavin' here with a breath of life in me. Can I?"

"We will not spend this entire time here talking about death," said Miss Whitecastle. "Do you understand? I won't hear of it in this house."

"Yes ma'am."

Maxine rose from the dining chair, picked up her bag, and proceeded toward the small den off the sleeping porch where she typically slept when she helped ready the cottage.

"No, Maxine," said Miss Whitecastle. "I've set you up in the front guest room."

Maxine turned slowly and stared at her employer.

"The one with the big window that takes up the whole front part of the room? The one where you can see all that's going on out there on the beach? Are you sure? Now you know it don't matter to me where I sleep. I'm just happy to be here."

"Well, why don't you just take your things in there and I'll heat up some of that soup I brought for our dinner."

eighteen

"Take off your wet clothes and find a place to hang them to dry," said Daniel. "You can wrap up in one of those blankets to sleep." Then he disappeared behind some hay bales to strip off his own clothes, leaving Rose shaking in the glow of a lantern.

Rose was hesitant about taking off her wet clothes. She was 11 years old and in an old, falling-down barn in the middle of nowhere with some older man that her mother liked, for some reason or another. There were probably snakes and rats and spiders in the barn. Her friends would never believe all this. She did what she was told, however. She figured Daniel must have her best interest in mind or he would not have gone through all the trouble of saving her on the river.

The wet clothes clung to her, making it difficult to pull them from her cold, damp skin. Her shaking hands were not much use. The bathing suit clung to her torn back. She bit her lip, controlling her tears. She was certain the constant rain beating on her all day had somehow permanently penetrated her bones. She sneezed. She wanted her mother.

The thin, unkempt woman had at least been kind

enough to bring some worn, but dry, blankets to the old barn, along with the lantern, a few biscuits, and some water.

"Ya need to be outta here as soon as the rooster crows," she said as she was closing the barn door. "I'll hold him off 'til then. Just get back on that path and follow it on until you reach a real road."

"There's a place to sleep over here," said Daniel from his hay bale dressing room. "Bring the lantern over with you."

Rose's body felt heavy from exhaustion. Her muscles, sore from the earlier struggles in the river, throbbed. Rose wrapped one of the blankets securely around her at the neck and made her way over to where Daniel sat – also tightly wrapped. He had spread out the remaining two blankets over the flat area of several hay bales laid side by side, making two lumpy, but adequate beds, for them both.

"Here's a biscuit," said Daniel, thrusting it toward her. Then he added, "Hopefully it's not filled with some kind of concoction that will lull us into a deep sleep so she can boil us alive for her dinner." He laughed.

"Very funny," said Rose, not amused.

"Just kidding," said Daniel.

Rose nibbled on the stale biscuit and took a few sips of the tepid water. She was too tired to care about food – and too uncomfortable. Even though she was bound up in her blanket cocoon, she felt exposed and vulnerable. She wanted to be home, safe in her mother's arms.

The thin blanket provided little warmth. Rose was embarrassed by her constant shaking. Taking long, deep breaths, she silently willed her body to stop.

"You'll warm up as soon as the food hits your stomach good," said Daniel.

After several minutes, the shaking slowed. Gradually, Rose lay on her side against the hay bed and began to relax.

"We'll get back tomorrow," said Daniel. "Promise."

But Rose was already in a deep, exhausted sleep, lulled by the rain drumming against the tin roof.

nineteen

"Why weren't you ever married?" Maxine asked Miss Whitecastle boldly. It was early the next day. The two women were walking slowly along the beach toward the north end of the island, the high tide not affording them much space between the slope of the dunes and the spray of the water. Miss Whitecastle had hesitated when Maxine insisted they take the walk. Never had Maxine expressed an interest in traipsing down the beach during their past visits to Pawleys. She would stare off at the beach and remark how "glorious" it was, but that was it.

Miss Whitecastle was glad it was early. So far, she had not seen anyone she knew, and only a few joggers who did not seem to give the pair a second glance. And here Maxine was asking such a personal question, thought Miss Whitecastle. She pretended not to hear her. Maxine asked again, this time louder.

"Why ain't you never been married, ma'am? I know it's a personal question and all. But thinkin' that I might not get too many more chances to find out these things, I just figured I'd go ahead and ask. Don't you ever just wonder what them poor, poor folks in those New York buildins' wondered about when they knew they was goin' to die? I imagin' them stuck on the stairs or squished on an elevator knowin' the end was near … thinkin' it might be the actual end times. I'd be askin' some questions. Yes ma'am."

"I have no doubt," muttered Miss Whitecastle under her breath.

"I'd just want to know a little more about my fellow workers or my boss. I'd want to know about their life before we all didn't have no more life. I'd want to know, 'specially, if they was goin' home with me or not. Lord, I never cried so hard as I did when I saw that plane hit that building … saw those people jumpin'. Poor souls. I thought to myself, I need to be gettin' ready for Jesus cause if these ain't the end times, I ain't been readin' my Bible right."

"Yes, it was so very tragic," agreed Miss White-castle, glad that Maxine's mind was diverted from an interrogation about marriage.

Before they left the house, Maxine grabbed a Food Lion grocery bag off the counter.

"What's that for?" Miss Whitecastle had questioned.

"For my shells," said Maxine. "I can't go walkin' on the beach without pickin' up shells."

While she talked, Maxine stooped over often to gather shells and drop them into the flimsy bag. Often she would stop, wash the shell in the tide, and hold it up to let the sun gleam on the wet surface.

"Just look at them pretty colors … silver, peach, gray. He could have made them all black or all white, but no. He said, 'Let's put a touch a purple on this one, stroke that one with some blue, and add a little pink for my friend, Maxine. Pink's my favorite color."

Maxine held a white and pink ridged shell up for Miss Whitecastle to see. Miss Whitecastle noticed it was broken. She watched Maxine as she picked up mostly all broken shells. In Miss Whitecastle's hands were three well-formed, unblemished shells.

When the women reached the end of the island, they had walked about one quarter of a mile from the house. They stopped and watched kayakers crossing the channel to the Litchfield beach. A group of sandpipers perched, as if stranded, on a giant boulder at the jetties. The water crashed around them, but they seemed oblivious, preening their gray and white feathers.

Miss Whitecastle and Maxine turned around and began walking back. Maxine showed signs of fatigue. Her stride slowed and her breath quickened. Miss Whitecastle contemplated the scene that may unfold if Maxine were to collapse on the beach before they reached her house when Maxine squealed with a high-pitched girlish enthusiasm.

"Miss Whitecastle, lookee there!"

Near the shore, where the water waved one last time before gliding onto the sand, a mother porpoise was rolling and playing with her baby, who seemed fixed to her side. Their bond apparent, the creatures appeared oblivious to the nearby onlookers.

"Now that's a divine sight if I ever saw one!" said Maxine. "That's a picture!"

And as quickly as they made an appearance, the mother and baby dove in unison and became a spot on the horizon.

"Now weren't that somethin'?" said Maxine, grinning.

Miss Whitecastle feigned a smile. Behind it was an inexplicable yearning to skip into the tide and throw herself into the spray, allowing the salty water to purify her soul, letting all inhibitions wash out with the tide.

The urge passed quickly.

"Weren't that somethin'?" asked Maxine again, still searching the horizon for the dolphins.

"We better head back before it gets too hot," said Miss Whitecastle.

They were almost back to the house when Miss Whitecastle asked, "Maxine, why is it that you pick up the broken shells? There are plenty of beautiful shells on the beach. You don't have to pick up the broken ones."

Maxine smiled, as if she anticipated Miss Whitecastle's question.

"Why, I think I must feel sorry for 'um. I just think they remind me ... ain't our lives all broken up just like they are? We're all different shapes and sizes. Some of us are smooth. Some of us are all bumpy. Some of us are just down right flat. None of us is perfect. But we all got a beautifulness about us, just like these shells. That's why, ma'am."

twenty

"I don't mean to rush you, but you should probably get dressed so we can get started," said Daniel, shaking Rose's shoulders. At first, Rose was completely disoriented. She stared at Daniel and then adjusted her eyes to the interior of the barn. She heard the rooster crowing loudly and hoarsely. She had slept harder than she could ever remember sleeping.

"We don't want our kind host to greet us this morning," added Daniel, trying to rouse her.

"Okay," she managed, as she forced herself up from the hay. She was stiff and cold, and the thought of putting on damp clothes was agonizing. Daniel walked to the other end of the barn as she made her way to where her clothes hung on the sawhorse. He opened and checked his pack with his back turned while she struggled with her clothes, which had dried only a little during the night. It hurt to pull up her bathing suit over the wound.

Rose pulled her tangled shoulder-length hair out of a ponytail holder, tried to work out some knots, and pushed it back up into another ponytail. Her stomach growled loudly. After she dressed, she walked to where Daniel was waiting and offered a faint smile. He had saved the last biscuit for her. She ate it in silence, drank a few sips of the water, and announced, "I'm ready."

"Let me check your back first," he told her. Then, upon examining it, he said, "It's no better or no worse. As soon as we get back, a doctor needs to take a look."

They gingerly exited the barn. Daniel looked around for the gun-toting property owner. The clouds were low, and the rain had slowed into a droning sprinkle. The sky was overcast, a somber gray, but Daniel had a better view of his surroundings. He could not imagine how the inhabitants survived. The mud, filth, and stench alone, he thought, were enough to kill someone. The pigs and chickens lived in mucky pens right next to the makeshift home. Garbage was strewn around the yard. Daniel hoped they could leave the premises without disturbing the mutts inside. Quietly, they walked toward the primitive road.

"I feel like Dorothy," said Rose, in a peppy tone. "Instead of a yellow brick road to Oz, we have a muddy, ruddy path to who-knows-where."

"At least we have a path now," answered Daniel. "It's got to lead to somewhere. These people have to enter civilization sometimes."

"I bet it's not too often," offered Rose.

The night's rest energized Rose. Her mother had marveled, and expressed as much to Daniel, in the way her daughter could fall into a deep sleep anywhere – the floor, a chair, the ground – and wake up refreshed afterwards.

Once they were on the road and supposedly head-ing toward some useful destination, Rose felt compelled to talk, and to ask questions. At least it would help pass the time and keep her from thinking about dry clothes and good food, she thought.

"Are you from Mexico? Spain? It's just that your darker hair and skin make me wonder about it," she began. She did not wait for his answer, but continued instead: "There was this boy in my class from Mexico. His name was Jesus. I couldn't believe it at first. I didn't think anyone would dare to take the same name as God's son, but then I learned that it was not pronounced like we say Jesus. He had dark hair and skin, but he had an accent … you know, like a Spanish accent. He made the best grades in Spanish. The rest of us were just clueless."

"You're awfully talkative this morning," said Daniel, grumpily. He craved a cup of strong, dark roast coffee, preferably from Starbucks. He was in no mood to talk, or to get cross-examined by an 11-year-old. He just wanted to get home. He felt a twinge of guilt, though, for the way he had cut Rose short the day before. He had lain awake much of the night imagining what Julia must be thinking happened to her only child. He just wanted to get Rose back safely … forget about the whole ordeal. He wondered whether he would ever dare take anyone rafting again.

"I know you don't have an accent or anything," Rose continued. "Maybe your parents were descended from Spain or somewhere. We learned about geneol … genealogist … I mean genealogy, in school. It's where …"

"I know what it means," said Daniel. "My parents adopted me as a baby. I don't know who my birth parents are."

"Gosh," said Rose, pondering his pronouncement. "That was a long time ago ... like 50 years or something, wasn't it? Mom said you were about 50."

"I'll be 50 in a few months, yes."

"You never found out who your birth parents were?" said Rose, puzzled.

"I tried to, once ..." started Daniel. It was 20 years ago, exactly. He considered it his "dark time." Something in him had motivated him to the point of near insanity to find the answers. For years, friends and then colleagues had questioned his heritage. In fact, he found it surprising that the senior partner at his firm was the only one who never inquired about it. That he secured a plum position at the firm at such a young age, with only top grades and no experience under his belt, made him somewhat suspicious. He convinced himself it was dumb luck. Still, he deeply desired to know where he was from; to have some idea who his real parents were and why they put him up for adoption. It consumed him. He had spent hours, and a good deal of money, looking for answers.

His adoptive parents evaded him whenever he brought up the subject. His mother always sobbed; then laid on the guilt trip. "Haven't we been good parents to you? Haven't we treated you well and given you everything you wanted and needed. We love you," she would cry.

Daniel would gently explain that he just longed to know, that it would not change his feelings for them. It was a void that, once filled, would give him peace, he reasoned.

His parents would appease him with vague

answers: "It was some attorney. We didn't get his name. They didn't require all the paperwork like they do now …"

It was not until he demanded to know, after every nerve ending yearned for the knowledge, that they relented. "I have a right to know where I came from and who I am!" he yelled at them. "If I have to completely find out on my own, you will lose me for good!" His mother had left the room sobbing, and returned with a piece of paper bearing the name of North Carolina Children's Services.

"I thought you said an attorney handled it," he scolded.

"An attorney was present during the signing of the papers," said his mother, sadly. "He held you while we signed the papers."

"I tried to find out, once," Daniel finished telling Rose, "but it didn't work out. I just gave up. It's not important," he lied.

He remembered the crushing weight of disappointment and rejection – a full force blow to his stomach – when the social worker at the organization called him to say that the "other party" was not interested in making contact. The finality of it all was almost too much. He spent weeks moping, trying to put in all into perspective. A big, media-frenzy case – his first of such magnitude – pushed his personal life, his past, to the back burner, and that is where it stayed.

"I can't stand not knowing," said Rose. "My mom didn't ever want to talk about my dad after he left us, but one day I just told her I had to know. She told me the truth. She said he was from Spain. But for some reason I didn't get dark hair and brownish skin. They met when she was there doing a summer study abroad program or something. She liked him right away. Said he was so charming. He followed her back to America. They got married right away, or so she thought. Then she found out he had done something that wasn't quite legal in Spain. And when our government here started asking questions, she found out that something was wrong with the marriage license. Well, it's all very confusing. But anyway, he told my mom that he was going back to Spain to get it all straightened out. And I bet you can guess the rest."

"He never came back," said Daniel.

"That's right," said Rose, "and mom was already pregnant with me. So I never saw him. Not once. She doesn't even have a picture of him. I think I would like to at least know what he looks like … maybe even meet him. But then again, it's been me and mom so long that I just think it would be weird. Do you know what I mean?"

twenty-one

   Miss Whitecastle announced to Maxine that she would be "going out" for a while just as the home health nurse, Amy, was arriving. After a few weeks of fair health, Maxine began to slowly diminish and Miss Whitecastle felt it best to hire a nurse to check on her. For the past few weeks, Amy came twice a day, over from Georgetown, about 15 miles away. She checked Maxine's vitals, and made sure she was comfortable. When necessary, a small dosage of pain medication was administered. The cancer was beginning its invasion on internal organs. After one night of listening to Maxine moan exhaustedly from discomfort, Miss Whitecastle had called the physician in Columbia and asked for a prescription.

   When Miss Whitecastle insisted Maxine needed something to alleviate the pain, Maxine declared: "I want to know what it's like to die … want to feel it till the Lord takes me. I don't want to be in some la la land and not even knowin' when it's happenin'."

   Maxine relented, though, only when the pain was unbearable. It really only took the edge off; did not send her into a stupor of half-consciousness, or "la la land" as she put it.

Amy also helped give the weakening woman her daily baths, and generally just kept her company while Miss Whitecastle took a walk or feigned running errands.

Miss Whitecastle heard Amy enter Maxine's room.

"Amy, now ain't you a pretty picture," Maxine greeted. "Did you curl your hair? That looks so pretty around your face. Did you bring another one of your poems to read to me? I do like those. Yes, indeed."

Other than Miss Whitecastle, the nurse, and an occasional delivery person, Maxine had little contact with the outside world. She received a few cards from concerned relations or friends who learned where she was staying. She wrote them back a polite note saying she was "fine" and "appreciated the prayers." Maxine's two brothers had called more than once. Maxine spoke with them briefly the first time, but then refused to later.

"Maxine, you need to speak to your brothers," scolded Miss Whitecastle. "They must be so worried about you."

Maxine's response was curt: "They knew me when I was alive and kickin' up my heels. They knew me when I was their happy and lovin' sister. I'm dyin' now. They don't need to know me this way ... all tired out and puny feelin'. Tell them they'll see me soon enough in the glory land. I'll be doing some kickin' there, I tell ya!"

As she was gathering her purse and car keys, Miss Whitecastle heard Amy reciting one of her poems to Maxine. When Maxine found out that Amy was a believer, and a Christian poet at that, she whooped and declared that Amy better "share them poems. That's why God gave you the gift, after all."

Amy read:

"Unlock my heart as I fall on my face,
Take me to Your holy place.
As humbly I bow before your throne.
Unravel this web that I have sewn …"

"I'll be back soon," Miss Whitecastle called, as she walked out the door. Miss Whitecastle drove away from her Atlantic abode and toward the historic seaport of Georgetown, famous primarily for its establishment as the third city in the United States. She crossed the Waccamaw River, with its wide sweep of wild marshes. Exiting the bridge, she noticed an enormous osprey nest with overflowing contents in a man-made box on a pole that she assumed some conscientious naturalist must have erected.

She crossed over another bridge. Under her were the Black and Pee Dee Rivers that wound like snakes from the upcountry of South Carolina, to join as an estuary before traveling together to the salty sea some 10 miles beyond.

Entering Georgetown's tree-shaded streets, and passing the immaculate picket-fenced yards and freshly painted courthouse, Miss Whitecastle decided that the charm of the town would be a refreshing distraction from the looming death she left at her house. She parked on Front Street, directly in front of the florist. She made a mental note to buy daisies *to cheer up the place* before returning to Pawleys.

To the left of her parking spot was Georgetown's famous clock tower, situated in what was the Greek Revival marketplace at one time. The clock had kept time since 1845, even after the town surrendered to the U.S. Navy during the Civil War. Facades, like the one made of cast iron and looming black over the tourists who perused the stores, were lovingly maintained on this nostalgic street that skirted along Winyah Bay.

Shop windows were tall and presented the owner's flair for creative merchandising. Dogs often lounged at the entryway of open shop doors, or sat dutifully beside their handler at the cash register.

Miss Whitecastle decided to lunch at the Dogwood. She asked for a dockside seat, believing the marsh breeze would do her good. She watched the activity of the schooners and fishing boats maneuvering in and out of the narrow passage. She spotted a spaniel waiting patiently on the dock for its owner to unload a well-dressed woman in a fuchsia tank top and white pants. The sun warmed Miss Whitecastle, relieved her temporarily of the suffering that occurred inside her beachfront home.

A small alligator swam under the dock where Miss Whitecastle enjoyed a hearty bowl of she-crab soup. It startled her for a moment. She looked around. No one else noticed. It probably subsisted, she thought, off uneaten treats that the tourists threw to it up and down the waterway. She imagined it dining on chunks of po-boy sandwiches, hush puppies, and barbeque.

Miss Whitecastle felt emotionally ill-equipped to have a sickly woman living in her home. *What was I thinking?* And Maxine's constant questions, wanting to talk, annoyed her – made her think too much. She had spent her entire life concealing those bleak recesses of her life. She did not want them revealed. Yet, she could feel something … a strange gnawing inside her. It made her restive. She wanted to flee, wanted to back out of this impractical commitment she made to her dying servant.

When Maxine worked at Miss Whitecastle's Columbia home, she talked, certainly. But Miss Whitecastle felt she could let her drone on for hours without having to offer her full attention. During the first few weeks of their beach stay, Maxine rose in the morning, ate, went back to bed, rose at noon, ate, washed a dish or two, mentioned helping with some laundry or sweeping, wandered back to her room, and often slept through dinner. Her strength waned quickly, however. In the last two weeks, she seldom got out of bed without prompting and assistance. But often, while lying in bed, she would ask Miss Whitecastle to sit with her "for a spell" while she talked.

A boy in a tiny blue boat, powered by a small outboard motor, became dwarfed between two large recreational crafts. Miss Whitecastle noticed that several of the boats had Charleston and Savannah painted on them. They must have traveled to Georgetown for the day, she wondered, to experience the quaintness and slow pace of the smallish town.

The she-crab soup, subtly briny, but creamy and soothing, was welcoming to her soul, despite the rising heat of the day. She watched as a sports fishing yacht full of beer drinkers congratulated themselves, laughing and high-fiving on their boat, which was aptly named "At Ease".

A good catch? A good life? When had she last felt like celebrating, she wondered. *When Joseph asked me.* She believed it had all come together for her in that moment.

• • • • •

After a Sunday lunch at the Barrister's home, he
politely asked her to accompany him in the garden.
He sat with her on the cool wrought iron bench
facing the pineapple-topped fountain. He was shy,
but beautiful to look at. His blond hair curled just so
at the sides. He was pretty handsome, she remembered, not rugged like most men she knew. Not the
stretched, tight look of her father, either, but rather
soft, with tiny lines around his mouth that curved
upward when he laughed.

He spoke gently, with intent, not robustly and
proudly like his peers. When he conveyed a thought,
it was worth noting.

"Do you know that I love you, Ellen?" he said to
her, taking her fingers like they were feathers and
resting them in his palm. "I do," he added, without waiting for her answer. "You and I have been
connected since childhood. It's inevitable that we
should be joined for a lifetime."

He attempted to gaze into her eyes, but his shy-
ness prevented it. Her heart beat more rapidly than
it ever had or has since.

"I'll be 21 soon and finished with my education,"
he continued. "It's time we begin planning our wedding."

She does not remember saying, "Yes," but she
must have. He brushed her lips with his, much the
same way he had in the past – nothing passion-
ate, but tender. Passion would come later, or so she
thought.

"Let us tell our parents," he said, before she had time to fully absorb the moment.

"Let's Joseph," was all she could manage.

The days leading to their wedding date many months later, she recalled, were flurried with the chaos of appointments, meetings, dinner parties, portrait sittings, decision making, silver selection, and dress alterations. Rarely did she have time with Joseph alone. When she did see him, she glowed with a confidence she had not known earlier. All of Charleston seemed to have known this event would take place at some point in their lives. The engagement ring on her finger confirmed it for her as well.

She decided that she had always loved Joseph, even when rebelliousness once tempted her to go against this match that her father pre-ordained even before she uttered her first words. But her love for Joseph, because it was expected of her, had been tentative. Prior to the engagement, she did not feel free to really express the depths of her affection. Once he asked her to marry him, affirming his love for her and binding a trust between them, she was more compelled toward expression. But pre-wedding obligations prevented her from sharing her true heart. She planned to spend the rest of her life demonstrating her love for him. That had been her plan.

• • • • •

The next morning was Sunday. Miss Whitecastle paid Amy extra to come early so she could attend church. She fully expected to partake in the service at the historic and stately All Saints on the mainland of Pawleys, but an unexplainable urge drew her to

Pawleys Chapel. Formerly a Pentecostal Holiness Church in Georgetown, the chapel was dismantled and relocated in 1947 to become one of the island's historic landmarks.

Miss Whitecastle, with her attraction to fine architecture and imported stained glass – two "musts" for a church, in her opinion – felt strangely that the one-room chapel with its white painted wood siding and tiny steeple of a simple wooden cross, would comfort her. She stiffened, though, when she saw long-time Pawleys' acquaintances, Fanny Buford and Maddie Jane Neal, approaching the entrance. She thought about leaving, but they spotted her and waved. By this time, she felt like everyone must know she was caring for a black woman in her home. Even her Columbia bridge friends called to question her, disguising their disappointment at not being invited to her cottage as usual. Instead, they offered pleasantries and news involving their own summer adventures. They had "heard," probably from Columbia friends who dropped by while vacationing at their own Pawleys' homes, only to be turned away because "it was not a good time," that Miss Whitecastle was allowing her servant to die in her house. She knew they thought her peculiar, eccentric even. She would have liked not to care, but she did. So, she simply avoided them.

Miss Whitecastle took her time ascending the steps at the church, to make certain Fanny and Maddie would have time to already seat themselves. The small structure was barely grounded at the entrance. The rest of the church jetted over the marsh and was raised just a few feet above high tides by pilings. Amazingly, the marsh water only threatened to rise and seep through the floorboards into the sanctuary during hurricanes. When Hugo barreled through, the exterior of the church was heavily damaged. Miss Whitecastle and other "Pawleys Permanents" gave generously for repairs.

Two rows of wooden pews with a large floor-to-ceiling window behind the pulpit, afforded a broad view of the marsh. A painting of a smiling Jesus was the back wall's only adornment. Before she seated herself, Miss Whitecastle noticed a tall shaft of pure white in the window frame – an egret standing tall and firm in the wet grasses, tenaciously anticipating the arrival of breakfast. An earlier summer shower, as well as the high tide, filled the marsh so that the greenish brown grasses were only visible at their tops.

Two young men took their seats beside Miss Whitecastle. She guessed they were in their late teens or early '20s. One had wavy blond locks, while the other was dark-haired with chiseled Greek-like features. They sat closely, too closely, she thought fleetingly, to one another. She shuttered.

The choir, which consisted of three women, a keyboard player, and a guitarist, asked the congregation to rise. They led the summer visitors in a song unfamiliar to Miss Whitecastle, "My Redeemer Lives." One line of the song struck her, "I will rise with Him."

Will I?

She was pondering this when the visiting preacher, from a Baptist Church in Georgetown, began bellowing about God keeping his promises. Miss Whitecastle glanced over at the two beside her. They seemed to be listening to the service. She diverted her eyes to their hands.

Has God kept his promises to me? Did I ask Him for anything? Have I ever?

She realized later that it must have been her imagination, but it seemed that the preacher turned his focus onto her and began directing his sermon toward her – for her benefit.

"You haven't asked for his help! You have pride!" he boomed. "Heaven's not worth missing so you can say to yourself, 'I did everything on my own.' Jesus can rescue us from being held captive. Something has happened to you that you can not forget, or forgive. So you're stuck. Stuck!" he thundered.

Miss Whitecastle stared, mesmerized.

"But Jesus can save you from it," he continued. "He can save you for a new, changed life … to help others. Don't live less than what God wants you to be. You're destined for more than you're living now."

Entranced, the spell was broken when it seemed that the pastor took his eyes off her, glanced around at the others, and then bowed his head for the closing prayer.

She stood for a moment following the prayer, feeling the full weight of the pastor's words. The congregation in the tiny chapel came alive with the energy of exiting the space. When she turned and bent to pick up her purse, she heard the dark-haired boy say to the other, "See you later, Joe."

twenty-two

"Do you hate them?" asked Rose.

They had been talking so much that Daniel did not realize it was already mid-morning. Initially, he had decided to placate her. He attempted to remain somewhat guarded, imagining her sharing every detail of their conversations with her mother. Gradually, he found himself sharing more with this young girl than he had with most women he had known. She had a maturity and an uninhibited nature that put him at ease.

"Hate who?"

"Your birth parents. Because they didn't want to see you or get to know you. I think I might hate them."

"Hate is kind of a strong word, don't you think?"

"No. I sorta hate my dad for what he did."

"Well, I don't hate my birth parents. I'm very hurt and disappointed, I guess, but they must have had a reason for doing what they did. Your dad probably did too."

"I guess. Can we sit down for a minute? My feet are really hurting."

The longer they had been walking, the rockier the

terrain had become. In places, it was steep and slippery from the mud. Large stones and deep, water-filled ruts created an obstacle course on the road. Daniel could not imagine how anyone could get a four-wheel drive jeep, much less an ancient junk heap, up or down that road.

"Certainly," answered Daniel. It was the first time she conveyed even a hint of a complaint. *She's a trooper, I'll give her that.* He knew she must be hungry.

They walked off the road to where a large boulder, fairly flat and cracked perfectly down the middle – probably from some small seismic wave thousands or even millions of years ago – was worn smooth from centuries of pounding rain. *It's amazing what water will do to stone, given time.* Spread across a vast section of the rock was a blanket of rich emerald lichen. A thick shelter of evergreens provided them almost complete relief from the ongoing drizzle.

"We'll rest here for a little while," said Daniel, sitting down in the area that was lichen-free. "Sorry there is no food." Then he offered, optimistically, "We'll surely be back by dinner time!"

It was closing in on noon. Daniel was perplexed as to why they had not discovered other homes, or heard any signs of human life. He knew that where Jon pulled the raft out the day before was fairly remote, but not nearly as remote as he was finding the Western side of the river, where he and Rose were stranded. The Western side of the French Broad seemed a world unto itself. A few times during their walk down the road, Daniel noticed a thin line of a trail leading into the dense wooded darkness. For a split second he thought of investigating, thought

that maybe others lived along the road that hopefully led to the world beyond. But he thought better
of it. It was more likely they would walk up on a
bear trap or an old still than find some friendly soul
to help them.

Daniel laid back on the rock and Rose followed
suit. Soon they were both asleep. Daniel awoke
45 minutes later to a whirring sound overhead.
He jumped up. Rose heard it too. He stood up on
the rocks waving his arms and shouting. But the
canopy of trees covered them too well. The helicopter paused only for a moment in the area above the
rocks, then flew Southward along the river. Daniel
looked toward the direction of the river. He suddenly thought of pushing back through the expanse
of green labyrinth that stood between him and the
river. He thought that if he could find a clearing near
the river, the helicopter pilot may be able to spot
them.

But he quickly deflated, knowing it would be
asking too much of Rose; and besides, there were no
guarantees that all the areas along the river would
not be flooded over. The whirring noise moved
away from them. Daniel decided they would continue to stick to the road. He was encouraged that at
least someone was out looking for survivors.

"Let's go," he said to Rose.

"But, but …" she started, looking up at the sky.
Daniel could see that she might cry.

"There is no way they can see us here," he assured
her. "Our best bet is to keep walking. If we see a
clearing, we'll look for the copter again. Otherwise,
we'll just stay on this path. It's leading downward,
off the mountain. I have a feeling we might end up

near Hot Springs, which is a small town along the river."

Daniel's words mollified Rose. For a short time, they walked in silence. She seemed sullen, to be pondering their fate. Then her demeanor changed. She seemed, abruptly, to have all but forgotten about the helicopter.

"Why haven't you ever been married?"

"You certainly are an inquisitive thing, aren't you?" said Daniel. "And why do you think that's any of your business?"

"I just think it's strange that someone your age has never been married."

"My age ... Now listen, Rose ..."

"My mom says it's probably because you see divorces every day ... that you probably don't believe in marriage. Is she right?"

"You seem to have all the answers. What do you think?"

Rose thought for a minute. "I think that your heart's probably been hurt so much and that you've probably seen other married people being so mean to each other that you just don't want to have any part of it. That's what I think."

"How old are you?"

Suddenly, Daniel stopped. He grabbed Rose's arm. He held her firmly where she stood. Both stiffened as a large black bear lumbered toward them on the road. She was lifting her nose high in the air, sniffing her surroundings. Daniel determined immediately that it must be a female looking for her cubs. She did not seem to notice them, but was instead searching around her, throwing her head from side to side. She appeared desperate and disoriented.

From what he read, he knew that animals, as much as people, were affected by flashfloods. Often wildlife would lose offspring, shelter, and food in the destructive waters.

Daniel held Rose's arm hard and mouthed to her to stay quiet and still. But her wide eyes foretold hysteria. Without warning, the mother bear fixed her eyes on them, raised up on her back legs, and growled low and foreboding. Rose screamed and pulled from Daniel's grasp. She began to run in the opposite direction.

"No, Rose! Don't run!"

It was too late. He had no choice but to run after her. The fleeing humans ignited the pursuit instinct in the bear. With the full force of her 250-plus pounds, she charged at them. Daniel caught up with Rose and threw her to the ground, covering her with his own body. In predictable black bear fashion, the bear came near enough to be frightening and then backed off from her intimidating charge. She pawed the earth, roared, and shook her head.

Rose wrenched herself from Daniel's grasp, stood up and tried to run again.

"Rose, no! If you stay still, she won't ..."

As Rose turned around to judge the distance between her and the bear before sprinting away again, the bear took another opportunity to charge. Her mouth was open and she thundered toward Rose. This time Rose froze; horror registered on her face. She took one step, swayed slightly, and collapsed in a heap on the muddy ground. Daniel again threw his body over hers. More empowered, the bear did not stop and turn back. She sniffed hard at the bodies on the road, pushing at them with her wide snout. She swiped at Daniel's back with her two-inch claws. He muffled a cry of pain against Rose's limp body. The bear sniffed again, then growled loudly at its victims. Feeling no threat, the bear backed off. Daniel lay, perfectly still, listening for the bear. As she trudged off, she growled in short menacing bursts. It was not until he heard her crash through the woods that he pulled himself, and the wilted form of Rose, up off the road.

twenty-three

With a few hours remaining before she expected Maxine to need lunch, Miss Whitecastle planned to find solace from her unsettling morning by watching CNN in her room. The current world's news of war in Iraq would distract from the preacher's words earlier, and from the image of the two boys on her pew.

No sooner had she entered the door, however, when she heard Gidget's too-long nails clinking toward her on the cedar floors. She needed to go out. Miss Whitecastle passed by Maxine's room and was surprised to see the door open.

"Maxine?" she called, wondering if Amy had taken her to the bathroom. She could not recall, in fact, if she had even seen the nurse's car still parked in the driveway. No answer. She came back out into the large living area and found Gidget whining at the back door. Miss Whitecastle went to the door and saw Maxine sitting in a rocking chair on the deck, covered with a light throw. The early morning rain left a slight chill in the air. Wind rustled around the few palmetto trees that surrounded the deck.

Maxine sat, conscious only of the breaking sea

beyond. She appeared deep in thought. She did not turn to acknowledge Miss Whitecastle when she stepped onto the deck, but perked up at the sight of the little dog, who jumped up to place its two front paws on her blanketed lap.

"Maxine. Where is Amy?" asked Miss Whitecastle.

"Oh, I sent her home. No one needs to work too much on the Lord's day," Maxine answered. "I knew I'd be just fine 'til you got back."

Maxine rocked slowly back and forth, contemplative. She stared off at the white elephants, made large and foamy by an offshore storm. A flock of willets flew up and down in unison over the waves, landing for only a moment before the next wave came. Thick dense mounds of bubbles piled up on the shore, a phenomenon caused by crashing salty waves.

Then Maxine looked at Miss Whitecastle.

"How was your service this morning, ma'am?" She spoke in a groggy state.

Not wanting to be reminded, Miss Whitecastle said, "Fine." Then, "Are you hungry?"

"I could eat. In fact, I was just sittin' here wantin' a taste of some frogmore stew. Hadn't felt much like eatin' in days and days, but I got me an appetite today. You know how to make frogmore stew, ma'am?"

"I haven't made it in a while, but yes, I believe I could make it. I have some shrimp and red potatoes in the refrigerator. I can run to the store for the sausage and corn. Mr. Perkins at the Town Hall was selling some of his tomatoes yesterday. He might be there today as well."

"Make sure you smell 'um."

"I will."

"Now I don't want to cause you any trouble about the stew," said Maxine. "If you want to make …"

"No trouble, Maxine."

Miss Whitecastle opened up the deck gate to allow Gidget to descend the stairs and do her business in the sandy yard. Miss Whitecastle turned to go back into the house, intending to check the cupboards before venturing to the market.

"Miss Whitecastle, ma'am, I almost forgot. Amy said you got a call from your brother Charles while you was at church. Said it was important that you call him back right away."

Charles rarely disturbed her while she was at the beach. But when he had learned that she had taken Maxine to the beach with her for an indefinite amount of time, he was appalled. He telephoned her and grilled her about her intentions, never hiding his ongoing disappointment regarding her inability to make good decisions.

"How can you show concern and compassion for her when you can't even do the same for …"

She had stopped him dead. "Don't you even," she warned him, letting his words dangle and then fall. *The gall of him.*

The more he challenged her now – and pretty much throughout their lives – the more she dug in her heels. He sometimes reminded her too much of her father and she did not want to be forced to yield to his standards.

Reluctantly, she called him at his home in Charlotte. She braced herself for more of his badgering. He answered after the second ring.

"Charles, is anything wrong. If it's about Maxine …," she said, already defensive.

"Have you watched the news?" he asked her.

"No Charles, why?"

"He's missing," he said.

"Charles, who's missing? Slow down."

"*He's* missing." He let the full weight of the words hit her before he continued. "And the reason it's on the news is that he has a high profile girl-friend and her daughter is missing too. Some kind of rafting accident in the mountains. I just wanted you to know from me before you saw it on the news. They are showing his picture. You would recognize him if you saw the picture."

"How, Charles? I've never …" She felt light headed.

"Trust me, you would know his face."

"Charles, why are you telling me this? I told you long ago not to ever mention it again. You know it is not to be spoken about." She realized the hand that held the telephone receiver was shaking.

"I just thought you would want to know, Ellen. For God's sake … I know you don't want anything to do with it, but I thought at least … oh, forget it. I just wanted to give you fair warning in case you turned on the news. Good bye."

Miss Whitecastle sat for a long time with the phone receiver to her ear, staring at the wall in front of her. When the phone began to make an obnoxious beeping noise, she lowered the piece onto its cradle. *Why is this happening? Is it not enough to have a woman dying in my home?*

She fought against going to her room and turning on the television. But curiosity eased her toward the set and convinced her to push the "power" button. She felt a yearning to finally know … to see for herself. Already, the channel was on CNN. Sports news was ending. The reporter announced the top stories would be next. She waited. She sat, dazed, at the edge of her bed. She picked up the remote and turned the television off. She immediately turned it on again. *This is ludicrous.*

The top stories reported more car bombings in Iraq, Condaleeza Rice's visit to the destitute country, then a follow-up on Prince Charles's marriage to his long-time mistress, Camilla. A story about extreme flooding in parts of Tennessee, Kentucky, and North Carolina segued into a piece about a rafting guide and one of his passengers, the 11-year-old daughter of a promising new fiction writer, who went missing after flash floods swept through several rivers around Asheville. They showed the photograph of the author and her daughter first – most likely a publicity photo, thought Miss Whitecastle.

Then they showed his photograph. She gasped. Charles was right. She did recognize him. And somehow she knew; she always knew that he would look exactly like him. The photograph left her television screen and she faintly heard the reporter say something about sending out a search party. But Miss Whitecastle was already stumbling toward the bathroom, her tattered insides heaving with her own disgust. She fell toward the toilet, bruising her knees, hugging the bowl, and wanting the water to suck her into its depths. *It's too much.*

Self pity and self loathing depleted her. She was a wretched person, with a wretched past, and a lie for a life. She decided she was staying there, on the bathroom floor.

"Ma'am! Ma'am!" cried Maxine. "Ma'am! Ma'am!" Maxine was wailing.

Miss Whitecastle had completely forgotten about Maxine – forgotten about grocery shopping, lunch, the frogmore stew.

Miss Whitecastle forced herself up off the floor, grabbing the towel bar for support. She struggled to her feet. Maxine was carrying on relentlessly.

Miss Whitecastle found her still sitting in the rocking chair. She was rocking hard and crying. When she saw Miss Whitecastle, relief spread over her face.

"Oh, Lord save me," she said. "I musta slipped off for a while and when I woke up my legs didn't wanta work. And when I asked for ya, you didn't answer and I thought I was all alone out here. I couldn't remember where you'd gone to. And I just got scared, ma'am. Forgive me," she said, still crying. "I just got me a case of the heeby jeebies."

She grabbed Miss Whitecastle's hand, clutching it hard. "Can you sit with me for a few minutes?"

"Maxine, why don't we go inside? I'll take you in and get you comfortable in your room."

"Amy said that if I just sit a little while and stretch out my legs slow like, that they'll start workin' again. It's just on account of that pain medicine that my legs go to sleep and it don't feel like I can wake um up.

"Just sit with me a minute," she said, insistently, still clutching Miss Whitecastle's hand. Her crying subsided.

"Well, I need to, uh ...," Miss Whitecastle tried to protest. Her insides were still queasy.

"Oh, please, ma'am. Take a load off your feet and

mind," Maxine urged. She began to stroke Miss Whitecastle's hand with her thumb, rubbing it back and forth along the top. Miss Whitecastle sat down in the rocking chair next to Maxine, who concentrated on the sea. Miss Whitecastle felt strangely comforted. She acquiesced to the black woman's strong, but gentle touch.

"I haven't thought about my daddy for a long time," said Maxine, still staring ahead. "You ever wonder why I hadn't mentioned him? I rattle on and on about my momma, my brothers, and my sister, but I've just kept my daddy all locked up like he's servin' some long prison sentence."

Miss Whitecastle knew Maxine's sister had died as a young girl. Something Maxine had said years ago made her suspect her father as causing the death, but Miss Whitecastle could not remember why.

"I've been so mad at my daddy for so long. And now I'm sittin' here sick and dyin' and wonderin' how a soul can stay hatin' for so long. I've just been hatin' him for killin' my sister, Bethany – straight from the Bible – and for killin' himself."

Miss Whitecastle sucked in her breath. Maxine heard her and said, "Oh yes. That's what happened. He worked at that Otis Repair Shop fixin' farm tractors and trucks. My daddy could fix anything … guess that's where I get it. He comes drivin' up in our driveway one day all proud and sittin' up high with a mighty grin cause Otis let him drive home a brand new truck that just came in off the 'ssembly line. Daddy'd never driven anything that new or fancy before. Never did after that either. He wasn't lookin' out for little Bethany 'cause he musta figured she was in the house with momma. But she came runnin' out to greet her daddy. She just didn't know to be afraid of cars or trucks. Just like a dumb dog, I guess. Ran right in front of his tire.

"Daddy fell out of that truck just a hollerin'. He picked her little body up off the driveway and screamed like I ain't never hear no one person scream. I was screamin' and cryin'. Momma came out of the house screamin'. My brothers ran down the road to get the doctor. There wasn't nothin' anybody could do. She was dead."

Maxine talked and stared off at the horizon.

"My daddy left after the funeral and didn't come back. Didn't pack a bag, didn't say good bye, nothin'." My momma just told us he had gone away and wasn't comin' back – and he didn't. My momma cried and cried, for what seemed like a year. She was in love with that man. She used to tell me, before he died, how he had seen her on the road one day talkin' to her friends when he and his buddy were headin' toward the river to fish. He said, 'Just a minute, I gotta go meet the girl I'm goin' to marry.' His friend said, 'Naw, come on. We goin' fishin'." He told him, 'Just give me a minute.' Well he talked to her all the rest of that day, and they never did go fishin'. Momma loved that story. Made her feel special.

"Well I just imagined, the rest of my growin' up years, that my daddy was out there walkin' around in a state of sadness, and that one day he'd come walkin' back down that driveway, ask for our forgiveness, and be our daddy again. But he didn't. I'd sit on the porch in the summertime at our two-tone green house with greens that didn't even come close to matchin', and I'd watch those morning glories all twisted around the porch railins'. I'd watch 'em start closin' up around lunchtime, and they'd be open again next mornin'. I'd sit there and just wait. Had a feelin' he'd come back in the summertime when the glories were bloomin'. Don't know why. Never did come though. Just sat there waitin' and he never did come.

"Then one day when I'm a teenager, I'm ridin' around with some girl friends. This one new girl who was stayin' down the road with her grandmother because her parents were fightin' was in the car with us. When we passed the Motel Goodday, she says, 'Is that where they say that man shot himself with a gun?' Well my friends, they gave me a look, and my best friend Bessie, she shushes her. And I say, 'Why are you shushin' her? What does a man shootin' himself at the Motel Goodday have to do with me?' No one says a word. They just look at me all sad-like, and I just knew. I jumped out of that car, ran all the way home, and almost took the door off the hinges of our house hollerin' and cryin' at my momma. I said, 'Why didn't you tell me my daddy shot himself at the Motel Goodday?'"

Miss Whitecastle looked over at Maxine. Fresh tears made wet, straight lines on her face. Miss Whitecastle sat, immobilized, unable to respond.

"My momma said he shot himself the next day after my sister's funeral. She made the whole neighborhood swear not to tell me or my brothers. Said it would've upset us too much. Said she wasn't lyin' to us when she said he wasn't comin' back. Guess she was right about that. But I was still mad at her for a while. Then I grew up and knew she was just protectin' me. It's easier to be mad when you're hurtin'. Don't know why. But, oh Lord, lettin' that mad go feels so much better."

Maxine broke from her sea gaze and looked over at Miss Whitecastle with tear-stained eyes.

"You still not told me why you didn't get married, but that's why I never got married. I said I ain't never goin' to get a heartbreak from a dead husband or a dead child. Now don't get me wrong. I love children and I love men. But my heart couldn't take that kinda hurtin'. Just couldn't."

She shook her head and turned her gaze again toward the vastness laid out in front of her. Miss Whitecastle tentatively reached her free hand over toward Maxine and rested it on top of the hand that she still held tight in her lap.

twenty-four

Daniel walked along for what seemed like hours, drained; his arms were aching with the weight of someone else's daughter in them. The sting in his back from the bear scratch was almost unbearable. He wondered how deep it was. A light fog had settled into the area, giving the already dismal road a murky glow. The rain was a steady mist now, tickling his face. He so wanted to reach his hand up and wipe his face free of the minute droplets, but he could not. He could feel that the top straps on his Tevas had rubbed his skin and were finally cutting into his wet feet.

But mostly he was worried about Rose. Her head thudded lifelessly against his chest, keeping time to the rhythm of his cadence along the rocky path. Every now and then a low moan exited from her mouth, but her breathing was steady. Other than that, there had been no real movement in some time.

Daniel fully expected that after he picked her up off the road and carried her to an area a safe distance from where the bear had attacked, that she would quickly come to. He had scooped some rain water that gathered on an indented rock into his hand and wetted her forehead. He had called to her, rubbed at her arms, checked her pulse. He tried sitting her up, then standing her up, hoping to jolt her back into consciousness. But she stayed out. He felt her fainting so quickly was mostly from the bear charging toward her, but also from overwhelming exhaustion and little food.

When he took river safety courses taught by trained emergency medical technicians, he remembered covering unconsciousness. Unless a person received a blow to the head or long-term exposure to the frigid water, typically they would regain consciousness in a short amount of time. Rose did not. This led Daniel to believe that fatigue and hunger probably exacerbated her condition. Still, he was not certain. The longer he walked, the less certain he became. As malaise set in, his mind wandered into the "what if" zone.

What if she's really dying? What if we have to spend the night out here again? What if we aren't rescued in time? What if that mother bear comes back?

Each time Daniel heard even a slight rustle in the thickets of mountain laurel, he stopped and tensed, ready for a new encounter with the grieving mother bear. Once it was a complete family of otter – father, mother, and two offspring – much farther from the river than he had ever seen them. They loped out of the thicket and down the same path on which his tattered Tevas had just tread.

Another time, the noise was a Great Blue Heron, hiding injured in the protective hedge and wildly flapping its mammoth gray wings about in an effort to get balanced.

Daniel hugged Rose tighter to his chest. He

thought, perhaps, that his body heat would warm her to consciousness. "Rose. Rose. Wake up," he tried, for at least the hundredth time. Nothing.

Fear began to squeeze at Daniel's heart and wrench at his insides. He did not know how to care for this girl. *I'm an attorney, for god's sake.* He imagined carrying Rose to the end of the road, finally discovering some semblance of civilization – an old country gas station, maybe. Some old guys in dirty overalls would be sitting on the covered front porch of the establishment, talking about the devastation brought on by the flash flood. They would stare at him like he was Jesus coming off the mountain. He would look down at Rose, then up at the men, and mouth the words, "Help me." One of the aging men would speak up and say, "It's too late for helpin' that one sir. She's gone."

He shuddered at his vision. His mind was foggy from exhaustion. Still, he pressed on. Daniel thought about what it must be like to hold an infant in your arms for the first time. Did his birth mother ever hold him, he wondered. His birth father? He doubted it. When he thought of his father, he imagined him in a far off place. His mother, though, he always considered close by – just slightly out of reach.

When his mother let the adoption agency know that she was not interested in establishing contact with her son, he reasoned that she was either completely heartless or so poor – and now feeble with age and probably poor health – that she could not muster the energy to visit a mistake made so long ago. The latter scenario was easier to live with. For as long as he could remember, his mind's made-up story of his adoption had been that his parents were extremely poor unmarried Mexican workers, and devoutly Catholic. This last part accounted for the fact that they could not possibly ever face their families back home with a baby out of wedlock. The Mexican part accounted for his dark looks.

The agency would give him no further information. It was a sealed adoption. Either birth parent had to agree to make contact before the agency would set something up. The agency told him that there were no records on his birth father.

Daniel heard a whirring sound that seemed to be just above the fog line along the treetops. He stopped. A helicopter. It was moving slowly toward the river. Without hesitation, Daniel placed Rose down where he stood; his arms were shaking from her constant weight. He turned and crashed through the dense underbrush, thrashing and tearing at the plants to get to the river. He threw his full body weight at the thick wall of rhododendron, depleting his last shreds of energy. The curving branches and thick leaves cut at him, but he was unaffected. His ears listened desperately for the position of the helicopter.

Instead of exiting the thicket onto a rocky beach, Daniel found himself standing on a mammoth boulder. He suspected that the boulder normally jetted out from the cliff and was several feet above the river. The flood had altered the water level to such a degree, however, that now the boulder was a part of the river, with water rushing around one side.

Daniel frantically waved his arms before he fully steadied himself on the rock ... before he sighted the helicopter. It was moving slowly up the river, undoubtedly searching for survivors. No. It was a TV helicopter, realized Daniel. As it came closer, he could see the call letters plastered on its side. A camera man hung slightly out the large sliding door, gathering footage of the flooded river for the evening news. Daniel saw the camera aim his direction. Yes! He yelled, "Help us!" at the top of his lungs, knowing full well that they would not hear him. He could see the others in the helicopter scrambling to figure out what to do. The craft was close enough that Daniel saw the pilot pick up a phone.

After a few seconds of hovering, the camera man put down his camera and held up a sign. It read: "SENDING RESCUE. STAY THERE." Daniel nodded wildly several times. The camera man picked up his camera and filmed Daniel for another few moments. Then the helicopter continued making its way up the river. An old windowless flatbed pickup truck floated by. Daniel watched the surreal spectacle, waiting for the helicopter to be out of sight before hurrying back to get Rose. He knew that if he turned to leave when the helicopter was present, the crew might think he would not be there for the rescue helicopter when it arrived. They had no way of knowing another survivor lay on the cold ground a few hundred yards away.

Daniel struggled back through the undergrowth. His shirt tore open on one jagged branch that he did not see until it was too late. It left a thin red scratch across his entire mid section. He broke back through, farther up than where he had entered. He ran to find Rose where he laid her. She was wet, dirty, and still unconscious. He wiped off her face, called her name again, and then picked her up. His arms bore the 80 or so odd pounds less securely. His body had weakened significantly in the plunge toward the river. He knew he needed to muster more strength to make his way back through, gingerly this time, so as not to further injure Rose.

He walked up the path and tried to find evidence of his exit from the bushes. The leaves and branches seemed to have snapped back into place, daring him to tread through them once again. He made a new entrance, listening intently all the while for the helicopter. A few times he had to pass Rose in between branches and lay her on the ground, only to pick her up again when he worked himself through the woodsy maze. Now and then Rose would moan or whimper in his arms. The task was slow and tedious. Daniel's heart rate quickened at the thought of not being on the boulder when the helicopter arrived.

Suddenly, Daniel stepped into cold water that tugged at his ankle. He was standing on the river's edge. He looked upriver and realized he had missed his target. The boulder was up several more feet. Frustrated, he thrust himself back into the thicket. A branch scraped the side of Rose's head. Her eyes opened wide.

"We're almost there. We're almost home," he said, as much to himself as to the child in his arms.

A large yellow tangled mass of rubber blocked his path. The raft had been compressed into the branches of an especially large rhododendron by the force of the river's fury. On its way down it had been ripped almost unrecognizable by the trees and debris carried downward with it. Daniel felt, almost certainly, that it was his raft. He decided not to work around the raft on the thicket side, and instead stepped slightly back out into the rapidly moving river. For a moment, it seemed he would lose his footing on the slippery rocks.

With one foot in the river and the other on a slight embankment at the very edge of the thicket, Daniel struggled toward the boulder. When he finally reached his destination, he laid Rose on it first, then pulled himself up. She was awake, but did not offer to move. He sat down, spent, and pulled her into his lap, cradling her like a large baby. He leaned her head into his neck and whispered to her in a smooth, steady tone, "We're going to be all right now. We're going to be just fine. We'll be just fine … just fine ..."

Daniel felt her body move and he turned her face toward his. She was staring, wide-eyed, fearful. Suddenly realizing the river flowed directly beside them, she gasped. Daniel held her closer. "Shhhhh. We're going to be just fine. Be still. A helicopter is coming to rescue us. Be still. It's going to be okay."

He stared at her, relieved. She relaxed in his arms. She hurt all over, felt tired and weak, but safe. "You know, you're not so bad," she said to him, smiling.

After several minutes of holding Rose on the rock, Daniel heard the approaching whir of the helicopter. They spotted him and Rose on the boulder. One of the crew waved from the window; Daniel waved back with his one free arm. He stayed, seated, on the rock, as a rescue worker was lowered down from the hull of the helicopter.

He smiled and yelled to Rose, above the rumble of the noisy blades, "You're not so bad yourself!"

twenty-five

From her bed, Maxine called to Amy, who was readying herself to leave from her daily visit. Maxine whispered something in her ear and then crammed a crumpled bill in Amy's hands before glancing at her door to make certain Miss Whitecastle was not eavesdropping.

The next day, the nurse whisked by Miss Whitecastle in the late afternoon carrying a large heavy bag.

Miss Whitecastle looked up from her reading, "What's that?"

"Oh, just something Maxine asked me to get," offered Amy quickly as she slipped into Maxine's room. The effervescent nurse proved an ideal match for Maxine's spirited nature.

Maxine awoke from her dozing. From her bed she commanded, "Lock it!"

Puzzled, Miss Whitecastle rose from her reading chair and tried to enter Maxine's room.

"Amy, why is this door locked?" she said, annoyed.

"I … uh …," struggled Amy.

Maxine answered for her: "Got somethin' goin' on

in here, that's all."

Miss Whitecastle stood at the door. Her brow furrowed.

"Amy, please open this door!"

"Ain't you never been surprised before Miss Whitecastle?" asked Maxine from behind the closed door. Then, to Amy, she smiled, shook her head and said, "Lordy mercy!"

Miss Whitecastle pondered this before settling back down to her reading.

The nurse and her patient giggled behind the closed door. *Maxine certainly is spunky today. What could they possibly be doing in there?*

Miss Whitecastle recalled Maxine coming to her home one Saturday years ago after she had lunched with the Red Hat Society. Maxine explained that her cousin, a longtime honorary member, had invited her to their organization's special spring brunch. The only stipulations for attendance being that "you'd better" dress your Sunday best and "you'd better" wear a red hat.

"Oh, we hooted and hollered and carried on so," shared Maxine. "I almost peed my pants. You should have seen us. All dressed up and taking up all these tables pushed together at the Red Lobster. We was a sight to see."

Almost peed my pants, indeed.

And then, after hearing a particularly loud outburst of laughter from the two behind-closed-doors collaborators, Miss Whitecastle thought, *Is anything really that funny?*

Feigning disgust, Miss Whitecastle grabbed Gidget's expandable leash off the hook by the door and announced loudly that she would be taking a walk. She found the dog lounging in the sun on the deck. Gidget was never too fond of touching her feet to the sand at the beginnings of their walks on the beach, but she always forgot her aversion to it once Miss Whitecastle allowed her off the leash to chase the sea gulls and sand pipers. Occasionally she would spot a fiddler crab, dash for it, and bark angrily at its hole – the poof on her bobbed white tail wagging furiously.

Miss Whitecastle walked an unusually long time. The sun began to make its quick departure on the horizon, spreading a silvery pink along the surface of the glassy water. Two dolphins sprayed and floated so near the shore that she caught their dark eyes now and then as they rolled around in the calm surf.

Miss Whitecastle came across a few shells so perfectly shaped that they seemed to beckon her to pick them up. But she had no desire to collect shells. The intimate moment she had shared with Maxine on the deck was on her mind. She knew that although Maxine seemed to have a burst of energy with Amy, she generally showed more signs of fading. She still managed her cheery disposition, but she slept much longer, and was not interested in getting out of bed except to relieve herself – and that required help.

Since coming to Pawleys, Miss Whitecastle knew the dividing lines between them had slowly began deteriorating. She sensed it in the way Maxine would poke fun at her, and pry into her private past. Maxine seemed to grow bolder the closer she got toward death.

One recent evening, Maxine yelled for Miss Whitecastle to come into her room. Frantic, Miss

Whitecastle thought the worst.

"You have to see this!" said Maxine, pointing at her television. "What is wrong with their brains? Why would anyone with a brain the size of a pea want to get inside a tank with a bunch of swimmin' rats? Can you tell me?"

"Oh, Maxine," said Miss Whitecastle, clutching her chest. "Why do you watch those dumb reality shows? Why don't you change the channel to the public broadcast station?" She moved toward the television. "There has got to be something better …

"No! Wait! I just want to see real quick if that crazy girlfriend of his jumps in there with him. What some people won't do for love. It's just not right. When I was gettin' on up there to the age when girls start gettin' boyfriends, I would of run faster than a jack rabbit if a boy wanted me to even touch a rat, much less swim with um.

"What'd you ever do for a boy, Miss Whitecastle?" she added.

"What do you mean, Maxine?" said Miss Whitecastle, suddenly feeling embarrassed and irritated.

"I mean crazy; somethin' crazy you wouldn't do 'cept you liked someone and it didn't seem crazy when you were doin' it."

"I can't recall doing anything crazy," she answered.

"Oh, Miss Whitecastle. Now I know you must a been in love sometime. Weren't you ever in love?"

"I don't wish to discuss it," said Miss Whitecastle, as she turned to exit Maxine's room. "Can I get you anything?"

Ignoring her, Maxine said, "My first love was a boy named John Elders – John-John, we called him.

Oh boy, was he a cute one."

Miss Whitecastle paused at the door while Maxine continued.

"I was a fool over him, I was. I was 'bout 16, and all the girls had their eyes on John-John. Well some of those girls started talkin' 'bout him after school one day while we was watchin' football practice. And John-John, he's just over there runnin' with the other boys. Those girls said, 'He likes me.' 'No, he likes me.' They were just a fussin' over which one of them he liked best. Well, I couldn't stand it because I wanted him to like me best. So I up and said, 'I know for a fact he likes me best.' They said, 'How you know?' I said, 'Watch this!' And do you know I walked right over to that boy where he was practicin' with all those football players and I gave him a kiss right on the cheek! Lordy mercy, what a stir. He just smiled and waved at all those girls standin' there with their jaws hangin' open. He started datin' a pretty girl named Pricilla soon after that, so I kinda got the wind knocked outta my sails. But that was a crazy thing I did. A fine moment, but crazy, you know what I mean?"

Miss Whitecastle turned to leave the room again.

"Oh, Miss Whitecastle, I think you're just keepin' the good stories about your boyfriends from Maxine. Someday you gotta tell me some."

When she made her way back to the cottage, the sky was dusky and Gidget was falling behind. *She's tired.* The house was quiet. She listened for Maxine's television, but heard nothing. She had not turned on her own television again since watching the CNN report. She couldn't. She hoped he was okay, but she could not bring herself to watch again. The photograph haunted her. It was better just to try not to think about it; that tactic had worked her entire adult life.

After she cleaned her feet of sand, she slipped into the house and peaked into Maxine's room. The light was on, but Maxine had drifted off. Amy was gone. A note was on the dresser. "Be back tomorrow morning. Call me if you need anything – Amy."

Miss Whitecastle walked closer, checking Maxine's breath. As Maxine's cancer deteriorated her, Miss Whitecastle grew more leery of the day when the breathing would stop. She turned to leave when Maxine's voice startled her.

"How's the beach tonight, Miss Whitecastle? Are we goin' to have a storm?

"It's very calm and peaceful," answered Miss Whitecastle.

"I can feel those ocean breezes comin' through the window. Amy made me stand there at the window and suck in that air a few good times today."

"That's nice. Are you hungry?" asked Miss Whitecastle.

"No, not really. Body's not really interested in food lately. Would like a good tomato, though."

"I'll check tomorrow at the vegetable stand to see if any farmers brought them in."

"It's gotta smell good."

"I remember."

Miss Whitecastle made a move to leave the room again.

"You know, they found that man and that little girl that got washed away by that flood in Asheville," said Maxine abruptly.

Miss Whitecastle's breath stopped short.

"You hear about that? It was on the news channel. Handsomest man and that poor little girl. That momma musta been worryin' herself to death."

"Are they dea …"

"No, they's alive. Thank God for that. They showed that momma waitin' for her baby when that helicopter landed. She just ran up to see her girl, who was on a stretcher, and she held her hand and was cryin'. And that handsome man, he just put his arms around that momma. He looked like he was just so relieved and happy. It's amazin' theys alive. You couldn't pay me enough money to live in them mountains. If you ain't got snow and ice in the winter, you got floods or landslides in the summertime. No ma'am. Not me."

Miss Whitecastle was suffused with relief. She did not realize, until that moment, how much she had been holding onto. She had tried, tried so hard, not to think about it, but it was with her every moment. *How could it not be?*

"Good night Maxine," said Miss Whitecastle as she left the room. She pulled the door half closed and stood with her hand still on the door knob. She paused. She walked back to Maxine's bed and sat down in the slip covered arm chair next to the bed. She sat there, hands in her lap, for several moments. Maxine remained quiet, allowing for Miss Whitecastle to contemplate her next move.

"Maxine. You know how you asked me the other night if I was ever in love?"

"Yes, ma'am."

"Well, I was. It was a long time ago."

"Was he a boy you were plannin' to marry?"

"Yes."

"I figured. I said to myself, 'A lady as nice as her musta had a heartache at the chapel or sometime right before never to get married.'"

"It is ironic. Now that I am thinking about it," said Miss Whitecastle, surprised at the assured tone in her voice; somewhat dismayed at the frankness with which she was about to expose herself to Maxine. "My heartache did happen in the church, but it was not right before or during a marriage ceremony."

She stopped and looked at Maxine, whose eyes were wide with compassion. A desire had been swelling in Miss Whitecastle for days. She could feel the words now, pushing their way up through her chest and into her esophagus – yearning to reach her vocal cords, aching to break free. Maxine was her safe place. "Joseph and I grew up together," she began slowly. "He was my father's best friend's son. We played together when we were little. When we got a little older, we talked to each other about books. He liked to read. He knew my father did not really want me reading all kinds of books, so he was discreet when he talked to me about them. When he was about 21 and I was 19," continued Miss White-castle, dryly, "he asked me to marry him. My parents were very happy. Since my father was president of a bank and I was his only daughter, he wanted to give me a wedding that 'Charleston would remember,' as he put it. Joseph was from a family who had owned plantations and still owned a lot of land in South Carolina. My father said the Barristers were one of the only families to come out of the Civil War and the Depression practically unscathed because they were so smart about their money. They owned one of the largest shipyards in Charleston when I was growing up, and Joseph was next in line to inherit and run it. My father said I would be well taken care of."

Miss Whitecastle stopped, suddenly seized with the dreaded reality of what she was doing; not sure if she wanted to continue.

"You go on now," Maxine coaxed her. "Think of this as your purgin' time. You got stuff in there that's just burstin' to get out."

Miss Whitecastle looked at Maxine and breathed deeply.

"A few weeks before the wedding, this family with some relation to Spanish royalty, arrived. They were acquaintances of the Barristers. They came to visit America and wanted to use the Barrister's guest house as their base while they traveled. But Mr. Barrister convinced them not to rush off, but to take in the sights of Charleston and the low country so they could attend our wedding. He told them they would be experiencing the best of true Southern tradition.

"Their eldest son, Manuel, was the same age as Joseph. He had dark hair and dark eyes, and was extraordinarily handsome. All of my friends thought so. They clamored to meet him. But he seemed like a rogue to me right away. Well, he and Joseph instantly became friends. They went everywhere together, it seemed. Instead of making preparations with me, Joseph was showing Manuel and his family around the city. He took Manuel out in the boat to Fort Sumter; he took him over to James Island. He even brought Manuel to the fitting of our wedding rings."

She paused. "I instantly felt jealous of Manuel. Then I felt ridiculous for feeling jealous. Then I just felt ashamed. Before Manuel came, I had Joseph's attention. After he came, I had none of it. But I worked hard to make certain Joseph did not know that I was envious. I did not want him to think I would be a silly, petty wife who made up things to be upset about. I told myself that I would soon have Joseph to myself, and that he probably just needed to have this last bit of freedom and fun before getting married.

"But when we were in the same room together, at pre-wedding functions and such, he rarely even looked my way. He listened to every single word Manuel spoke and laughed at his arrogant humor. Manuel would look at me from across the room as if to say, 'He's not interested in you, you silly twit.' Joseph seemed oblivious to it all … to how it all must be looking. But truly everyone seemed so enamored with Manuel and his family … their royal bloodline and all. No one appeared that put out at what was happening.

"Joseph was so outgoing around Manuel … not as shy as he always was with me. He just did not seem himself!"

Miss Whitecastle punctuated her last sentence with an edge of anger. She felt the blood rising into her cheeks. She breathed deeply several times to strengthen and calm herself.

She told Maxine of working up the courage to confront Manuel. She decided she would tell him that Joseph was expected to spend some time with her as they prepared for their future union. She would explain to him about the intricacies regarding a true Southern traditional wedding; she planned to enlighten him about the ways of a real gentleman.

Without carefully evaluating the full measure of her plan, she seized the opportunity one day after she stopped by to see Joseph and he informed her that he was off to meet with his father at the shipyard about some new procedural instructions.

"Where is Manuel?" she had asked him casually.

"He's staying behind and reading while his parents tour Middleton Place Plantation today," he said, not meeting her eyes. "Later, I'm running him over in the boat to see the Morris Island Lighthouse."

Indeed, she remembered thinking. But she politely and encouragingly told Joseph to have a nice day. She spent the better part of the morning in her room nervously reciting what she would say to Manuel. When her mother left to play bridge at the Buckley's, she left the house.

She slipped through the Barrister's courtyard, down the moss covered stone walkway, past the fountain where Joseph had proposed, and to the black painted door of the sizeable guest house. Manuel startled her by opening the door before she could knock. He had seen her coming.

"Well, hello," he said in his thick Spanish accent. With a charming bow he added, "To what do I owe this pleasure?" She remembered his smile broad and cunning; his teeth were large and white. Right away every nerve ending told her she had made a mistake. She was too lady-like, however, to cause a scene. She would see it through.

He invited her in and customarily asked her if she would like something to drink. "Shall I make you some tea?"

"No," she answered. "I simply came to ask you a question. I would like to know why you are monopolizing all of Joseph's time? Do you not realize that we are planning a wedding? This is a very important time in our lives."

It had all come blurting out in a rush. She had tried not to sound rude, but she knew right away her words were not friendly.

"I'm sorry that you feel that way," he answered, smiling and unaffected. "Is this not the American way, to entertain foreigners? Would you like for me to disgrace my own country by rejecting his offers of hospitality? You are angry with me, senorita?"

"Not angry," she composed herself. "I just need some time with Joseph myself, you see. There are obligations … social engagements …"

"You are jealous?" he boasted, his smile large and conniving. He moved toward her, reaching out his hand toward hers. "You would like some time with Manuel as well? No?"

"No!" she uttered, yanking her hand away; but he took her hand back commandingly. "Let me show you something," he said, leading her toward another room in the sizeable guest house.

"What do you need to show me?" she asked.

"You do not trust Manuel, senorita?"

No. She did not trust him and felt she was being manipulated. Regardless, she did not stop herself, or him. Despite his nettling demeanor, he was, after all, from an aristocratic family.

He led her to the lavishly appointed formal sunroom on the back of the house. She quickly looked around at its brightly colored floral-print upholstery. Naively, she considered for a split second that he wanted to show her a treasured antique in that room. Yet, in one swift movement, Manuel both closed the door behind him and jerked her to him. She drew in a startled breath and protested strongly;

pushing at his chest with all the force that her slender arms could effect. She tried to slap his face, but he caught her thin wrist and held it firm in front of her, a glowering presence contorting his face. She uttered one insignificant scream before he covered one hand over her mouth. A tempest rose in her and she kicked, and flailed, and dug her nails into his weighty arms. Yet, it was no use. Within the time it takes for one to walk to the mail box or drink a cup of coffee, he had expertly shamed her forever.

She was dreaming, she assured herself. Even when she opened her eyes, the room seemed heavy with a dense fog. The ceiling blurred when she tried to focus her eyes on it. This was not real. It could not be.

When he released her and stepped away, he was smiling. She gathered herself amid swirling pain and nausea and stumbled for the door.

"You must love me and leave me?" said Manuel mockingly, as she made her exit.

He called after her, "Remember, you came here to me. They will not believe anything else you tell them, senorita."

She walked home rapidly, straightening herself as she went. On the way she looked at each storm drain along the sidewalk and entertained the thought of climbing into one. She would disappear and none of this would have to be dealt with.

She was relieved to find that her mother had not returned from bridge playing. She tore her clothes from her body as soon as she entered her room, and then drew herself a bath. She fought the urge to cry, but broke down in a quick burst of heaving sobs. She gathered herself again. She scrubbed at her skin until it burned. She felt polluted. She thought about telling someone, but knew in her heart that not only would no one believe her, but that it would unleash a scandal in the close-knit Charleston community that would never abate, no matter how many generations passed her by. Why had she even risked going there? How could such a thing have happened to her? She did not understand it … would never understand. She would spend the rest of her life not understanding.

After some time passed, something internal arose in her. She decided she would forget about it. This would not alter her plans. In a handful of days, she would be married to Joseph. Manuel would leave Charleston. Life would go on.

She dressed. Then she wadded the clothes she had thrown off and took them to the furnace. She watched as they burned into ashes.

Miss Whitecastle continued, steadily, yet visibly shaken, with Maxine looking at her intently. She began speaking much faster. She wanted it to be said and over with, once and for all.

"The next time I saw Manuel, he acted as if nothing had happened. I did the same. The Sunday before the wedding, I took my place in our family pew as usual. Joseph had been sitting with me since our engagement, which was customary, but I looked around and did not see him. My father sat on the end closest to the center aisle, as did all the men. Next to him on the inside was my mother, then my brother, then me. Joseph could sit on the opposite end of the pew closest to the wall.

"Directly before the church service began, Joseph – and Manuel – came to sit in our pew. Father gave them a look of disapproval. I think that even he felt Joseph was spending too much time with Manuel and not enough time with me. I just know he did. Joseph sat closer to Manuel than to me. Manuel did not look at me. Joseph only slightly turned his head and said, 'Good morning, Ellen,' before turning his attention back toward Manuel. He spoke to me as if I were one of the elderly women at the church that he was forced to show politeness! Every part of me wanted to scream at him. I wanted to cry. I vowed before God that after church I would speak to him and find out if he still loved me ... if, perhaps, he really did want to marry me.

"I did not get that chance because the most unusual thing happened," she said, almost in a whisper, slowing her speech. She stopped talking and seemed to be looking off at some distant place. The scene was unfolding so vividly in front of her.

"Manuel took his suit jacket off because it was warm, even though men were supposed to keep them on during church no matter how hot the weather. I watched as he draped the jacket over his lap ... and Joseph's."

She paused, thinking back, struggling for the right words.

"Something in me realized that the jacket was covering something so sinister, so inconceivable to me. I just did not want to believe such a thing ... did not understand that such a thing could really be. But part of the jacket slipped off Joseph's lap when Manuel sneezed, and I saw them ... holding hands. They ... were ... holding hands," she said, perplexed, as if she were learning about it for the first time.

"How could they? How could he!" she gasped,

swallowing a sob. "Joseph looked at me right then and he knew that I saw. In that moment it all made sense to me. But it also made no sense to me at all. Do you know what I mean?"

Maxine slowly nodded her head. She was mesmerized by Miss Whitecastle's tale.

"Joseph quickly pushed Manuel's jacket away and straightened up like he was listening to that pastor preach. Manuel acted as if nothing had happened. He just stared ahead. I felt so sick that I wanted to run out of the church. But I knew if I did that everyone would know something was terribly wrong.

"Maybe I should have!" she said, coldly. "Maybe I should have exposed both of them right there!"

Then she added, sadly, "But I said nothing. I said nothing about anything that happened. Nothing."

She looked at Maxine with wetness forming on her eyes. Maxine, her eyes welled with empathy, placed her hand over Miss Whitecastle's, who left it there.

"I returned home from the church service with my family. I did not say good bye to Joseph. My father noticed and gave me a harsh look. At home I announced that I was not feeling well and wanted to lie down in my room. I did not come down for Sunday lunch. Later that afternoon I heard my father in the parlor speaking to Mr. Barrister. 'What do you mean he has had a change of heart! I will not hear of it! Your son *is* going to marry my daughter!' Then I heard the door slam. His heavy footsteps pounded on the stairs and he burst into my room shouting, 'Ellen! Ellen!' He roared at me. He waved an envelope in my face and shouted, 'What is the meaning of this? What have you done to make Joseph change his mind? What? I demand an answer!'

"I told him, 'Nothing.' He grabbed my arm firmly and pulled me from where I sat on the bed. He put the envelope in my hands and said, 'Open that letter. I want to read what you have done to turn Joseph from you. Whatever it is, I am certain it can be undone.'

"My hands were shaking and it seemed like it took a long time for me to open it. The only words on the card were, 'I am sorry. Joseph.' My father exploded in anger. He grabbed me by the arm, hard, and drug me down the stairs and out onto the sidewalk. My mother stood at the doorway and did not say a word. 'Where are we going?' I asked him. 'We are going over there right now to make amends,' he said.

"I pleaded with him to stop, but he did not hear me. He took me harshly to the Barrister's front door. Their butler answered, but Mr. Barrister came quickly behind him. His face looked swollen with anguish. He said, 'I told you that I am just as perplexed by this as you are. But I cannot force Joseph to marry her. I have threatened him with disinheritance, but he will not budge. He said he cannot marry her under any circumstances. He is leaving tomorrow to spend the rest of the summer in Spain – to clear his head. I am very sorry.'

"My father descended those steps and walked home without me. He died later in the fall. I do not think he ever looked at me again after that day. Everyone blamed me. Joseph never returned from Spain. Everyone probably thought I drove him away permanently. That is why I moved away from Charleston. That is why I never married."

Maxine allowed for some silence to ensue between them before she spoke, clearly, with measure.

"Here we are Miss Whitecastle. Two old women who have let life just pass on by us 'cause we couldn't shake the past. We've been all caged up like some sad birds, when we could've been free. We ought to be ashamed of ourselves, I tell ya. Ashamed. It's time to let it go."

I am ashamed.

• • • • •

Miss Whitecastle sat with Maxine for a long time that evening, wanting to tell her the rest. She wanted to divulge the most painful part, but she could not. It stayed tucked deep within her. The pregnancy; the leaving for Charlotte the moment she realized, before anyone noticed. The hiding out in her brother's home for months. The lying to her friends and family, telling them she needed to clear her head, that Charlotte was her temporary place of refuge. The birth of her child; the quick adoption. Leaving immediately to attend school in Columbia; building a new life. But worst of all, it was her brother Charles's disdain for what she had done. He could not understand her not ever wanting to hear about or know about her child. He took it upon himself, instead, to look out for the child's wellbeing – anonymously providing the funds for summer camps, then college, then law school, and finally offering a choice position at his own firm. Of these things, she would never speak.

• • • • •

"Don't you dare take me to no hospital," said Maxine weakly.

Miss Whitecastle had asked Amy to step outside Maxine's door. Maxine had not eaten in almost two days. She drank only a minimal amount of water, but only after Amy or Miss Whitecastle coaxed her repeatedly. She had been backing off her diet for weeks and her face showed the strains of dying – the giving way of supporting flesh around her cheek bones and eyes. Now she had no appetite.

"She's dead set ... I mean, she's determined to stay right where she is," Amy told Miss Whitecastle.

"I know. But I also know she would be more comfortable at a hospital, or at least with Hospice coming in."

The two women discussed options for several minutes and then re-entered Maxine's room.

"I ain't goin' to no hospital," Maxine sputtered. "And I ain't taken no morphines. Please don't take me to no hospital or give me powerful drugs. It's my dyin' wish now to stay here and smell God's great sea. That's all I want ... to rest in peace. Now you won't take a dyin' wish from an old woman will ya'?"

Miss Whitecastle and Amy looked at one another. Miss Whitecastle rubbed her forehead. "No one is taking you to the hospital," resigned Miss Whitecastle. "You would simply be more comfortable ..."

"No. And I means it. No," said Maxine.

Although the cancer inside her drained her life force, Maxine still had enough drive to give Miss Whitecastle and Amy instructions.

"I needs all them windows open," Maxine told

them, when it was decided she could stay put. "Let that salt smell in here real good. If I knew it wouldn't crazy my relations or get the Pawleys folks all worked up, I'd have you drag my body down on the beach so I can die there really smellin' it and hearin' the ocean up close. I wouldn't mind another blanket too. Thank you so much. Would you bring me some extra pillows, please? Oh, you're so kind to me."

When Miss Whitecastle came into Maxine's room to relieve Amy in the evening, Maxine told her, "I know you means well with that pretty music on and all. But what I really wants to listen out for is angels singin'. I just don't want to miss that."

Miss Whitecastle sat beside Maxine, watching her fade in and out of sleep. Maxine would wake, smile big at Miss Whitecastle, and then drift off again.

"You are so sweet to me," said Maxine once when she awoke. "You're just so kind and so sweet." Then she fell back into her slumber.

Miss Whitecastle stared out the window, listening to the rhythm of the crashing waves. *You're the kind one Maxine. Not me … not me.*

"Oh! I can't wait!" said Maxine the next time she awoke. Her eyes were bright, and instead of looking at Miss Whitecastle, she was looking up. Then she looked at Miss Whitecastle and said, "I can almost see it. I'm almost there."

"Almost where, Maxine? How do you know?" asked Miss Whitecastle, desperately.

"Oh, honey, I know. I just know. I feel it. I made a promise to Him years ago and this is His promise to me."

Maxine looked at Miss Whitecastle and smiled.

She reached out for Miss Whitecastle's hand and held it.

"You will know where you're going too if you just fix your eyes on Him," she said softly. "He's wantin' to love you … to give you some peace in your soul … but you have to let Him. Give Him your bad and He'll love you so much that nothin' else will matter. And when it comes time, you'll know. You will honey. You'll know."

Then Maxine closed her eyes again.

twenty-six

Timidly, awkwardly, Miss Whitecastle made her
way to one of the back pews at the chipped white
and blue cinderblock Church of the Living Christ
near the Fair Grounds in Columbia. The church
interrupted a row of green, yellow, light purple, or
white clapboard houses along a quiet street. Picket
or chain-length fences kept dogs in the front yards
and strangers out. All the homes had fading tomato
plants staked along the side yards. And all the
homes had porches. Even the church had a front
porch.

"Meetin' and greetin'. That's what us black people
like to do," Miss Whitecastle recalled that Maxine
had told her one day.

Miss Whitecastle settled herself. She sat, rigid, on
the pew. She looked straight ahead, but she sensed
stares that were quickly diverted. *How can they not
notice me? I'm the only white person here.*

Many African American families entered through
the church doors. Several older women sat together
on one of the front pews, their decorative hats looking like halos over their dark heads. There was a
shuffling of children, from toddler age to teenagers.

Miss Whitecastle noticed two well-dressed men approaching her. She darted her eyes to her left and right before realizing that no one was sitting on either side of her and that the men must want to speak to her. *What do they want with me?*

"Hello. You must be Ellen Whitecastle," said the taller of the two men. "I'm David, and this is Jeremiah. We're Maxine's brothers."

Miss Whitecastle stretched out her hand to greet them. "It's so nice to meet you. Maxine told me so many wonderful stories about when you were children."

They all smiled at one another politely.

"Thank you for coming," said David. "We appreciate your kindness toward Maxine. We tried to come and get her when we found out she was sick. Visited with her a few weeks before she called even, and she didn't even mention that anything was wrong. Cincinnati has an excellent cancer clinic. But Maxine wouldn't hear of it. She said she was fine and didn't want us remembering her in a bad state. She never wanted to be a bother and never would take anything from anyone unless she was forced. She just always wanted to do for everyone else."

Jeremiah agreed. "She called us last week, though, and it just about killed her right then to ask us if we would settle her bills with you when she was gone. She said, 'I can't die knowin' I've burdened my friend with my troubles. Miss Whitecastle's been every bit an angel to me ... every bit.'" Jeremiah smiled warmly as he imitated Maxine's voice.

Miss Whitecastle suddenly felt a heaviness overtaking her. She fought it.

David added, "We're just mighty appreciative of

you taking her in and caring for her these last days. Here's my card. When you figure out her expenses, please let me know and we'll take care of them."

"Oh, no," protested Miss Whitecastle, pushing the card back toward his hand.

"I insist," said David. "It was her wish. I can't go against that now, can I?"

Miss Whitecastle realized the standing trio had become the center of attention in the confined, mostly seated sanctuary. All eyes seemed fixed upon her. She glanced around her, took the card from David, and thanked him.

"Thank you," the two brothers concluded in unison. David clasped one of her small, frail hands and held it between his two large ones. For a moment he made eye contact with her and smiled. He released her hand and walked to the front pew with his brother.

Miss Whitecastle shakily took her seat just as the organist began "Amazing Grace." She sucked in a deep breath and bit at her lower lip.

During the service, the rotund pastor spoke of Maxine's kindness. He recalled how she was always willing to reach out to her neighbors in their time of need. He expressed her firm belief in the Lord Jesus Christ, while low "amens" were conveyed all around. A few dabbed at their tears with handkerchiefs, while it was necessary for others to wipe under their arms and mop at their brows in the sweltering church.

When the congregation rose, Miss Whitecastle sensed relief. A large lump had formed in her throat and her stomach knotted with nausea. She was ready to leave. But instead of the pews emptying toward the door, they spilled into a processional line for the viewing of Maxine's casket. Miss Whitecastle realized a hasty exit would not be appropriate. She reluctantly took her place in line. Slowly, the line inched along, each person paying their last respects, reciting prayers, or touching the sleeve of Maxine's dress.

The person in front of Miss Whitecastle – who oddly did not seem to notice she had taken a place in line behind her – was a slender, attractive woman in a black hat topped with a small feather plume. She began to whisper to the woman in front of her.

"Wasn't she an odd bird? You know where she's been these past few months, don't you? At that white woman's house at the beach! Odd, don't you think?"

The woman to whom she was whispering nudged her conspicuously and threw her head in Miss Whitecastle's direction. She caught Miss White-castle's astounded expression, then turned her back toward Miss Whitecastle and proceeded through the line.

Maxine's casket was only a few feet away. Miss Whitecastle could make out the lines of her dress, but she could not see her face. As she approached, she stopped and stared in stunned silence. Leaning against Maxine's peaceful face was her old china doll "Annie." Lying on her chest, against the pleats of a white dress, were two gold coins.

twenty-seven

Even in early September, the residue of Columbia's broiling summer heat held on. Miss Whitecastle opened the trunk of her silver Mercedes and struggled to pull out the garden stone. It was too much weight for her weakening arms. *I really should have waited for A. T.*

But she had already decided where the stone would go. She did not want to wait. The previous night she pondered it for what seemed like hours, carefully placing the stone visually in each spot before moving it to another location for consideration. By morning she had decided on the backyard impatiens garden, the one that Maxine planted for her each spring for those 34 years – the one enclosed by the black iron border she found in a shop on King Street in Charleston. She would place it directly in the middle of this squared garden and she would ask A. T. to plant impatiens for her next spring. This thought made her chest heave.

Hunched over, Miss Whitecastle slowly carried the stone to her back yard. Her arms ached, but she was determined. Each step was an effort as she balanced the heavy stone between her arms. The rough edges scraped at them.

She would be able to see the stone from her sunroom window. She dropped the stone near the garden, just missing her foot. She brushed off the loose concrete dust from her hands, fetched her garden shovel from inside her shed, and returned to the garden. With care she dug a shallow, round spot just slightly larger than the stone. Though she was wearing a dress, she knelt down into the bed. The pine straw and leaves immediately picked her pantyhose.

With great effort she pushed the stone into the opening she created. The motion was slow and purposeful, almost religious. Once in place, she packed the cool dirt around the edges of the stone. Still kneeling, she gazed at each broken shell. Some were a coral hue; others were white and dimpled. There was one with a high sheen and a swirl of gray. *That one is my favorite.*

All of the broken shells carefully connected to make a giant heart that dominated the surface of the concrete stone. Miss Whitecastle studied it for some time. She ran her hand over the shells protruding from the hard concrete.

She then pushed herself up on her hands, turned her body, and seated herself on the stone. For a long time Miss Whitecastle sat. She smiled when she thought of Amy sneaking in supplies to Maxine's room to make the stone. The beads of sweat on her brow traveled over her eyelids and blended with the tears that began to glide down her cheeks.

Her friend was gone.

She sat on her new stone until she could no longer endure the heat. She thought back over the past few months, and of the many other intangible gifts that

Maxine had unintentionally given her.

Miss Whitecastle stood up and made her way back into the coolness of her haven. She sat down in her mother's chair and picked up the telephone on the side table. She dialed her brother Charles's phone number.

"Charles, I want to meet him. Can you arrange it?"

After a long pause of silence, her brother answered: "Uh … well … yes, Ellen. Certainly."

"Good."

THE END

SPECIAL THANKS TO:

- *Editor and friend Carol Medford*
- *The gracious and richly humorous Harrelson family who opened up their Pawleys' home and their lives.*
- *Faithful friend and gifted poet Amy Clawson, who shared "**Free At Last**" for this novel:*
    May your glorious light shine on me,
    To reveal the chains I cannot see.
    Chains that have bound me so I'm no longer free.
    I long for truth and You hold the key.
    Unlock my heart as I fall on my face.
    Take me to Your holy place.
    As humbly I bow before Your throne,
    Unravel this web that I have sewn.
    I'm ready to hear what You have to say.
    Take my life, Lord, have your way.
    Open my eyes to the sin in my heart,
    And cleanse me, allow me to make a fresh start.
    Thank you for such forgiving love,
    And abundant grace from Your throne above!
    As Your unfailing mercy falls on me,
    I praise You, my Lord, for at last, I'm free!
- *Edward C. L. Adams for his book, "Tales of the Congaree"*
- *The Congaree National Park*
- *Walter J. Fraser, Jr. for his book, "Charleston! Charleston! The History of a Southern City"*
- *A supportive family*

ABOUT THE AUTHOR

Deena C. Bouknight writes for national and international consumer and trade home furnishings, architecture, and decorating magazines, as well as for general interest and regional magazines.

She has completed a second literary novel, Playing Guy, which is represented by the David Shepherd Agency. Deena has published one children's book, *Our Wintry Day Walk* (Trafford), and was a contributor for *Portraits of Grace: North Carolina Churches* (Our State Books), *Humor for a Sister's Heart* (Howard Publishing), and *The Big Book of Christmas Joy* (Howard Publishing).

She teaches writing and literature at private schools, and provides tutoring and workshops for homeschooled students. She is on the board of Prosperity Project, an inner-city tutoring and mentoring program in Columbia, S.C., where she resides with her husband, Gary, adopted daughter, Madeline, and adopted son, Justin.

To contact Deena, email dknight865@aol.com or dknight865@gmail.com. Her website address is deenabouknight.webs.com.

Made in the USA
Charleston, SC
22 October 2016